SNAKEBIT

ABSOLUTELY AMAZING BOOKS

Habent Sua Fata Libelli

ABSOLUTELY AMAZING BOOKS

Manhanset House
Shelter Island Hts., New York 11965-0342

bricktower@aol.com • absolutelyamazingebooks.com

Library of Congress Cataloging-in-Publication Data
Beckwith, David
Snakebit
p. cm.

1. FICTION / Mystery & Detective / Cozy / General. 2. FICTION / Mystery
& Detective / Amateur Sleuth.
3. FICTION / Mystery & Detective / International Crime & Mystery.
Fiction, I. Title.
ISBN: 978-1-955036-90-0, Trade Paper

August 2025

SNAKEBIT

DAVID BECKWITH

ABSOLUTELY AMAZING BOOKS

Will and Betsy Black Books
by David and Nancy Beckwith

A Hurricane Conspiracy (Book 1)
A Calculated Conspiracy (Book 2)
A Narcotic Conspiracy (Book 3)
A Cosmetic Conspiracy (Book 4)
A Jamaican Conspiracy (Book 5)
A Ransom Conspiracy (Book 6)
A Cover-Up Conspiracy (Book 7)
A Demonic Conspiracy (Book 8)
A Treasure Conspiracy (Book 9)
A Cruising Conspiracy (Book 10)
A Nautical Conspiracy (Book 11)

•

Conclusive, All-Inclusive Confusion

Available at fine booksellers

AbsolutelyAmazingEbooks.com

CHAPTER 1

FRIDAY A.M.

Normally, Matthew "Ace" Booker would be either going to work or already be there on a Friday morning but today was different. He hadn't told his wife, Jo Ann, any differently when he left the house that morning. Jo Ann would find out soon enough about the changes the family would soon be facing when the shit hit the fan. Right now Ace just wanted some time alone to think and sort things out — as if there was anything to think out.

Ace had volunteered to drop Matthias, who they called Matty, off at the Bowes-Carlson Day School, one of Miami's most prestigious private secondary schools, where he was in the ninth grade. He had gotten Jo Ann to agree to pick Matty up that afternoon. He'd prefer to not go back over there to the school once the cat was out of the bag.

Thank goodness it's Friday, and I've got the weekend to maybe sort some things out, he thought to himself.

After he left the school, he thought about the tuition at Bowes-Carlson — and the family's reputation.

I guess those days are over. … The public schools were good enough for me, he mused.

Matthew's head was in the clouds. He was barely aware of the rush-hour traffic around him.

Matthew got on I95 where he knew he had better get his head of that cloud unless he wanted to get in an accident. On 95 he had to not only drive for himself but for everyone else as well. He had to be alert every second behind the wheel. People wouldn't hesitate to cut him off if they thought they could get in front of him. Everybody seemed to be tailgating. And God help you if you were walking in a crosswalk since people would turn right in front of you if they thought they could get away with it. Respect for other people simply did not exist. How different it was from the part of Florida where he was raised! His mind drifted back to earlier days.

Thank the good Lord, he'd be getting off of 95 at Florida Highway 41 and head west.

With a little luck and the creek don't rise in less than three-quarters of an hour I'll be in Coopertown, he mumbled to himself.

Ace was jarred back to the present by the bone-shattering music of a rusty car to the right of his gleaming black Beemer XM SUV.

What a piece of doggy dung! I wonder what gang they belong to.

It was old and had been made worse by cheap add-ons that probably came from Pep Boys or AutoZone. It had multiple mismatched hub caps and a broken suspension. The windows were down. He guessed that they probably couldn't be rolled up. The owner had invested at least twice the value of the car in a stereo system, which, while loud, was obviously hacked together and sounded like crap. He recognized the Latin boogaloo sounds of Bobby Valentin's "Use It Before You Lose It" blasting loud enough to be heard all the way back to Little Havana.

At least they're not playing that rap crap, he sneered.

Both men in the car wore Miami Heat baseball caps, what they called la viser de béis bols — of course, worn backwards. The driver was only partially visible since his seat was pushed back almost to the car's B-pillar, but Ace could see he was wearing a number thirty-two Heat jersey; his companion wore number thirty-three. He assumed that the twosome was probably Cuban, but they could have been Puerto Rican since they were listening to Puerto Rican music. Thank God, they looked a little too old to be gang members.

At least they have good tastes in jersey numbers — Shaq and Alonzo — two of the all-time greats, he thought.

A gap opened in the lane front of him, and the driver veered entirely too dangerously close to Ace in his rush to fill it. Ace hit his brake to prevent a rear-end collision, but the other car kicked up a rock that cracked Ace's windshield. He almost shot the other driver a bird but then thought better of it.

Thanks, asshole for hurting my expensive car with that junker ... Oh well, after today it might not make much difference anyway ... The company won't be making the lease payments on my car anymore, so bye bye Beemer. You were a nice toy while you lasted. ... Oh, well. ... Screw all of you ... every last one of you.

Finally he reached the highway 836 exit that passed through Little Havana. The ghetto cruiser took that exit as well.

Figures! This ain't my day in any way, shape, or form, he shook his head and mumbled.

He saw a gas station that served Cuban coffee and decided to buy a cup so that the noisy twosome could get well ahead of him. It had some of the flaky guava pastry the Cubans call pastelitos de guayaba that looked good, so he bought one of them as well. Ace's ploy worked, and he was able to drive the rest of the way in peace as he listened with the volume set at a reasonable level to "I Feel A Tequila (Coming On)" on his Gary Roland and the Landsharks CD.

Much better. Actually, a tequila would taste good about right now, he sighed.

When saw the familiar Coopertown Restaurant, he knew he'd arrived at Coopertown, population eight. Its only residents were the Kennon family, all of whom were direct descendents of the Coopers. The restaurant was a one-story ramshackle, reverse-board-and-batting building with a gas pump in front of it. A sign on the window said **OPEN**. Another sign beneath the window said **COLD BEER**. A third sign with a bold arrow announced where to go for airboat information.

Originally Coopertown was a Seminole Indian village occupied by Jimmy Osceola and a few Indians until Bob Cooper decided to convert it into Coopertown. The three Cooper brothers were a Missouri family who had migrated to the Everglades from Melbourne, Florida, looking for a better place to go frog hunting.

By 1945, Bob Cooper's small frogging airboat became an accidental tourist attraction of sorts when curious tourists began to stop by and offer to pay him to take them out on his boat. He decided to build a small passenger airboat to accommodate them, and he found himself now to be in the airboat tour business.

After that Bob's brother, Jay, built a fish and tackle shop that was also a gas station, and his other brother, Marion, opened a small stand to sell sodas, sandwiches, and frog legs to the airboat passengers. This led to serving complete meals — fried gator tail nuggets and catfish, and what he called the best (and only) hamburgers in town.

Word spread far beyond Coopertown about his down-home, Everglades-style cooking. The diner's celebrity visitors' listing became almost too numerous to list. It included Doris Day, Dennis Weaver, Burt Reynolds, Dana Andrews, Ron Howard, Ferlin Husky, Slim Whitman, Mickey Mantle, Billy Martin, Jake Scott, Chuck Norris, Kurt Russell, Mariel Hemingway, Raul Julia, and Beverly D'Angelo, just to name a few. The movies "Invasion USA" and "Mean Season" were shot there as well.

Ace parked his clean car next to a dirty pickup and reached into the backseat to get out his sea mist colored Igloo Tag Along Too cooler.

I'll take a leak and get some beer and ice and some Doritos to take out on the boat. Modelo ... might as well get a good beer since this might be my last trip for a long while.

He spoke briefly to Jesse Kennon, the owner. He had phoned ahead to ask Kennon to make sure he had a full tank of gas. Kennon reassured him that the boat was gassed up and ready to go. Ace headed over to the dock where he kept his two-seater airboat, *The Offshore Account*. He smiled since only he knew that the boat's name held more of a meaning for him than anyone else, including his wife, realized. No one was there. Just a well. He wasn't in the mood to make any more small talk anyway. Ace sighed as he untied his airboat.

Soon Ace was shooting across the Glades. He popped his first beer of the day.

To think that this once covered over 11,000 square miles. And there's over ten thousand islands. ... Whoa! ... And also, amazingly enough, it channels 1.7 billion gallons of water a day into the ocean. Man oh man!

He didn't bother to get out the Asset Alliance baseball cap he kept on the boat. As the boat picked up speed, it would only blow off anyway.

Shiiit! With their problems, maybe that'd be for the best.

What looked to a novice like miles of flat land was in fact extensive wetlands perfect for aquatic creatures, and an airboat was the only link to what dry hammocks and tree-covered islands were out there. Whereas the water was shallow, it was no place for swimming. Some days the wonder of it all made Ace's head spin when he thought about how the tides, the salinity, the wind, the moon phase, the depth, the bait, the currents, and the time of day all came into play. But today Ace was preoccupied with other things.

Ace had been around boats since he was knee-high to a bullfrog. His daddy and granddaddy both had been Gulf commercial fishermen up the state of Florida. They were simple, hard-working, marginally educated people — the backbone of America.

To this day, Crawfordville, the town Ace was born and raised in, remained one of Florida's best-kept secrets. It was still "Old Florida," the way Florida used to be before high rises and condos erased the beaches. To this day, there were still no buildings over three stories high. It had beautiful beaches where both people and pets were welcome to walk its fine, white, sugary sands; enjoy the beautiful clear waters of the Gulf of Mexico; and watch dolphins frolic offshore. Sometimes they seemed almost close enough to touch. Sea turtles still visited its beaches each year. Immense sand dunes lorded over the cape instead of high-rise condos. In the evenings, spectators were treated to spectacular sunsets as the sun went down over the Gulf. At night the sea oats seemed to dance in the moonlight as they were brushed by light ocean breezes.

Alligator Point, a narrow peninsula about twenty miles long, was about an hour east of Panama City and a couple of hours away from Tallahassee, Florida's state capitol. Crawfordville was the home for the St. Joseph Peninsula State Park and the neighbor to both Apalachicola and St. George Island.

Crawfordville's bay was laden with fish, scallops shrimp, oysters, and crabs, which had provided Ace's family with a living for two generations. Apalachicola Bay oysters were considered by aficionados to be the sweetest in the nation. The grouper, flounder, red fish, sea trout, snapper, pompano, and cobia attracted sports fishermen as well, keeping the charter boats busy.

Growing up, when he wasn't in school, Ace helped his dad on the boat, but his parents made it clear that getting an education was always to be their son's number one priority since he had always proven to be a good student. No one in the family had ever gotten a college degree, and they were determined that Ace be the first.

Most local fishermen's children wound up doing what their forebears before them had done, making a living from the Gulf, but times were changing. Overfishing and the high level of bycatch were endangering the oceans' ecosystems. Illegal fishing was raping and pillaging the wild. Foreign competition from loosely regulated parts of the world was on the rise. Bottom trawling was destroying the fishing beds. Pollution was exacerbating fishermen's problems. His parents wanted their son to do better. Jack, Ace's father, continued to do the only thing he knew how to do — fish. Martha, his mother, cleaned motel rooms and took in sewing parttime. They tried to set good examples for Ace morally as well. The family attended the Abundant Life Community Church on a regular basis.

Matthew managed to qualify for the Florida Bright Futures scholarship program that paid his tuition and fees and attended the University of Florida. His parents began to call him Ace after he got an almost perfect score on his SAT. The nickname stuck. His parents covered his remaining costs, and he graduated with an accounting degree and soon afterwards passed his CPA exams on his first attempt.

Matthew Booker became one of the prides of Crawfordville and Wakulla County — the local boy who rose above his humble blue-collar beginnings and made good in the white-collar world. Jolene Maxwell, the longstanding Clerk of Court and Comptroller for Wakulla County, saw Ace's potential as a political asset for her and despite his youth and lack of experience; she gave him a job working in her office. He made sure that she never regretted giving him a chance. He instituted systems and updates that made her office a technological model for other Clerk of Court offices throughout the state. He also became a regular speaker at civic clubs, charity fundraisers, and on other affairs, like local school career days. He made sure that he spread goodwill for his boss.

Ace became active with the eight-county Big Bend Chapter of the Florida Government Finance Officers Association and served on the FGFOA's Technical Legislative Resources Committee. It wasn't long before he was invited to speak at their statewide meetings and other conventions for public officials on the technological efficiencies he had brought to Maxwell's office.

Jack and Martha's long term goal had been realized. Ace, the nickname they had given him, seemed to be becoming more fitting than ever. Their sacrifices and efforts had not been in vain. Their son was a success. They could hold their head up with anyone in town and say with pride, "That's my son."

They became even prouder yet when Ace married Jo Ann Peeples, the daughter and only child of the owner of Crawfordville's only local bank, the Paradise Financial Savings Bank, and when their grandson, Matthias, who they called Matty, was born.

Ace's growing stature did not go unnoticed. It attracted the attention of Alpha Partners, a money management hedge firm in Miami. They made him such a lucrative offer to be their comptroller that he couldn't refuse accepting, and the Bookers were off to South Florida. With Ace to help them open doors, Asset Alliance began to manage and invest public funds throughout the state, including those in Wakulla County. Ace was promoted from being not only the firm's comptroller but became a partner as well and a member of their investment committee.

Life was good for the Bookers. They lived in a ritzy neighborhood, drove expensive cars, belonged to the right clubs, and enrolled Matty in the exclusive Cushman School. If the people of Crawfordville had been proud of Ace before, then, he was now a rock star in their eyes.

"I didn't think anything could possibly go wrong but look at me now. Today my whole world is about to turn in to a pile of shit," Ace shouted to an egret flying over the boat.

CHAPTER 2

Ace repressed his upcoming problems momentarily as his airboat, The Offshore Account, began to glide across the primitive Everglades. He fully appreciated the fact that airboats like it were more than just a mode of transportation. These boats were his safe haven and portal into and out of this otherwise hostile environment.

While the Everglades are unusual and beautiful, they are still nothing more than a massive bog. They had their share of boggy swimming or flying beasts, but also unexpected denizens like racoon, deer, and wild boar. Moorhens and coots moved just far enough away to enable Ace's passage and then scrambled to scarf up the grass shrimp and minnows stirred up by his boat's passage. He momentarily thought about how fifty generations of these marsh birds had shared the Glades with people and their airboats. It seemed to him that after all this time they seemed to understand his thoughts and know how much room he needed as he shared the marshlands with them.

The boat glided and slid effortlessly across the grass and dollarweed as he made his way towards a patch of open water. Small shad thrashed the surface as they fled from the bass chasing them from below the surface. Birds were feeding from above. He goosed the throttle as he slid up a bank and powered his boat to the very edge. The bow was idling at first as it hung off the bank over thin air, but then he cut the engine off completely.

Too bad I didn't bring a fishing rod. This would be a perfect place to fish, Ace thought.

His head momentarily spun as he thought about how the tides, salinity, wind, moon phase, depth, bait, currents, and time of day all affected his fishing outings. He also thought about how occasional cold fronts blasted through this area in the winter and made the water temperature an even bigger factor and often trumped anything else.

Briefly, quiet settled over the area, and the marsh's normal noise resumed as the arrival of Ace's airboat was accepted as being normal. The environment seemed to display little impact from half a century of sharing their home with airboats like Ace's since most airboaters are conservation minded and operated their boats in a manner that respected the Glades' wildlife and habitat.

He popped another beer and just stared all around him, occasionally seeing a water moccasin. Marsh rabbits and wild hogs became a bit more aggressive since he had invaded their space.

"Don't worry, guys. You won't have to share this fishing hole with me today. Too bad I won't be here for dusk later today, however, to share it with you," he said to no one in particular.

When dusk did arrive later, Ace knew that the shriek of eagles playing would give way to the trill of families of racoons making their way to the water's edge. Turtles would push off logs as the sun's warmth began to fade into the trees. Soon, the daytime sounds would give way to crickets and mosquitoes. Feeding gators would begin to splash, and owls would mark the daily shift change.

Ace recranked his engine and went over the embankment.

Is there something symbolic about me just going over that cliff?

As he once more glided along, he could see the reflective orange eyes of gators sink slowly away from him as his airboat-propelled sled slid by them.

Reminds me of some of the Federal agents I've met recently.

Ace had had no experience in dealing with Federal agents until recently and wished he could still truthfully make that statement. It began subtlety at first. He noticed a black GM sedan in front of him and another behind him as he took Matty to school one morning. The one in front of him had an official U.S. Government license plate. When they came to the school, it kept on going, but the one behind him turned into the school driveway but kept going past him without letting a child out. It also had an official U.S. Government license plate. Ace didn't give it much thought until it happened again the following day. The third day his car was flanked by two Ford Explorer SUVs. Both had official U.S. Government license plates.

Surely, this is a coincidence. Why would someone be following me?

He didn't have time to give it much thought as he drove to his office in the Southeast Financial Center building. He needed to get in and look at some notes on the material he was expected to be familiar with at the nine o'clock investment committee meeting, and he had promised to pick up a dozen donuts from the Dunkin' Donuts' drive-through on Biscayne Boulevard on his way in. He always got the same order — two glazed, two cake, two chocolate jelly, two vanilla jelly, two vanilla frosted, and two Boston crémes. He didn't have time to go in this morning. That done, he drove into the financial center's fifteen-story parking garage and parked in his designated spot. As he walked to the elevator, he noticed another GM sedan rounding the corner.

Or is it the same one? Hmmm! Black. Almost official looking. Coincidence?

Ace stepped into the elevator just as the car went by and turned just in time to see the license plate. He also was able to see the car's driver and passenger. ... A man and a woman ... both dressed in business attire ... conservative suits ... The man was wearing a tie.

And also an official U.S. Government plate!

The coincidences kept occurring.

A few days later, Ace went to the members-only Downtown Athletic Club that was located in the Southeast Financial Center building. As he shot a few baskets with a colleague, he noticed two people walking past the gym.

The same two people. ... but now they don't have business suits on but are dressed in gym clothes. What in the hell is going on?

Seeing what appeared to be Feds happened again and again over the course of the next month. Ace even imagined seeing their cars driving through his neighborhood. He began to get rattled, but he kept his thoughts and suspicions to himself both at the office and with Jo Ann at home. He certainly didn't want to sound like a nutcase.

This all changed one morning, however, when Ace was running ahead of schedule and decided to go into Dunkin' Donuts and get his hot latte along with his usual donut order since there was a long line waiting to go through the drive-through. A woman wearing a business suit he had never seen before was in front of him in line.

When it came time for her to order, she turned and said, "Mr. Booker, why don't you let me treat you today?"

She turned back to the clerk and said, "Give us two medium hot lattes and a dozen donuts. Pack the donuts to go. Make it two glazed, two cake, two Boston crémes, two chocolate and two vanilla jelly donuts, and two vanilla frosted. Did I get that right, Mr. Booker? Why don't you grab that table for us."

Ace was caught off guard and floored. He didn't know what to say so he complied.

She brought their order over to the table and said, "Mr. Booker ... or would you prefer I call you Matthew or Ace? ... My name is Agent Foster."

She pointed at the front door where another agent stood.

"That's the door and you can walk out of it right now if you so choose because you're not under arrest. ... But let me tell you before you take that option, that we know a lot of what you've been doing in your professional life. And let me assure you that the ripple effects from it will soon spill over and destroy your private life."

She paused and waited for him to speak. The dumbfounded Ace said nothing so after a silence that seemed like an eternity to Ace, she looked him straight in the eye and continued.

"And, let me repeat, you can walk out that door right this second, but in a few weeks you're going to hear a pounding on your door at six A.M. That is the anointed time that the FBI arrests people. If you wait until then, your window of opportunity to cooperate will have closed. However, if you answer our questions truthfully over the next few weeks and help us with our investigation, you will possibly save yourself from a fate that you don't even want to imagine."

Ace did not walk out the door. Agent Foster nodded and the man quietly joined them.

"May I introduce you to my partner Agent Douglas?"

And that was the beginning of Ace's unwanted involvement with the FBI.

CHAPTER 3

Ace Booker's employer, Alpha Partners, had truly begun very modestly. Now it was part of a several billion dollar diversified asset management firm that had been founded under the Midas Insight LLC banner by Steven "Skip" Shipman and Jin Woo.

Skip Shipman had begun his career in the investment industry as a trainee in E.F. Hutton's Miami office. Skip began to teach an investment class at St. Thomas University in Miami Gardens as a way to prospect for clients and build a following for himself. Some of the members of one of his classes became interested enough in investments to talk the rest of the class into forming an investment club if Skip would agree to be their advisor. One class member, Jin Woo, did business with ChemChina, a Beijing based chemical company. Using his knowledge of the chemical industry, the investment club succeeded in beating the averages by a wide margin on a consistent basis.

As word of their success spread, primarily because the club members and Skip both liked to brag, the club grew and became permanent even after the class was over. Their popularity especially seemed to spread in the Asian community. Woo introduced Skip to Asian investors for what was at first an under-the-table finder's fee. Skip later introduced Jin to his manager at Hutton and convinced him to take Jin on as a legitimate licensed broker trainee. The two became partners, and because of the money Jin was able to bring in from Asia, they became substantial producers. When Hutton was convicted of mail and wire fraud, Skip and Jin left the firm, set up Midas Insight LLC., and took their clients with them. They had now grown from being members of a small investment club to being the principals of a small investment advisory firm.

Flash forward. With the help of Jin's Beijing and other Asian connections, Midas Insight grew from being a small investment management firm to being one of substance. They were now a recognized player to be taken seriously by the industry.

Flash forward again. Now Midas Insight owned Alpha Partners, the private equity fund Ace worked for, as well as a division named Security Income Investors, that dealt with private and public retirement and pension funds, and Asset Alliance, an arm that managed smaller sums of money for the public at large. BHive Currency Traders, an offshore over-the-counter crypto trading desk, was incorporated as a separate corporation. Midas' assets under management now ran not in the millions but in the billions. Their tentacles reached out even farther than they disclosed to outsiders. Two separate offshore banking corporations in Singapore and Liechtenstein, owned in shell corporations formed by some Asian based Asset Alliance clients, provided custodial services for the corporation as a whole, on what appeared to be a transparent basis.

The various entities had not, however, gone completely unnoticed by the FBI.

****

As Ace drank yet another beer, he thought about the terrifying series of encounters he had had with the FBI since that first "chance" meeting at Dunkin' Donuts. They had enlightened him about things that they suspected were occurring within his own firm that he was either unaware of or had chosen not to notice.

They clarified for him their definitions of the charges of complicity, being an accomplice, and conspiracy and the dire consequences that would result if he were convicted of violating any of these laws — even if it was due to ignorance.

"Complicity is the participation in a completed criminal act as an accomplice or a partner in crime who aids or encourages other perpetrators of that crime and who shared with them the intent to complete the crime. Do you understand?" Agent Foster said.

Ace nodded. Agent Douglas then spoke up.

"Good. Now let me define accomplice. An accomplice is a person who knowingly, voluntarily, or intentionally gives assistance to another or fails to prevent this other person from committing a crime. Nod it that's clear."

Ace numbly nodded again.

"Now, finally, a conspiracy is when two or more people actively collude to commit a crime. And one last thought. An accessory to a conspiracy can be either before or after the act."

Douglas leaned in, invading Ace's space, and while looking at him with deadpan eyes growled, "If you force us to, we may go after you for all of the above. It's going to be up to you."

"And there's a good chance that you'll end up with the same punishment as the perpetrator," his partner added. "Have I made myself clear?"

Ace stumbled and stuttered before beginning to try to make excuses. He soon found it would be useless to try to convince them of his innocence if indeed any illegal events were really happening. First of all, neither of them cared. And on top of that, they couldn't believe that he was really as in the dark as he claimed to be.

The agents elaborated over and over how deeply they suspected Midas Insight's relationship really was with the Chinese Triad.

At last, he began to fully understand Alpha Partners' phenomenal growth from a small local investment advisory service to being both a multinational hedge fund and a traditional investment advisory firm as well.

Foster and Douglas told Ace specifically what information he was expected to provide to them if he had any hope of staying out of prison. He had complied. He also began to make preparations with secret plans that he discussed with no one including Jo Ann.

Today was to be the day that the FBI would invade his office, confiscate their records, and arrest the officers of the firm. That was why Ace was out on his airboat instead of being at work. He'd already gotten his secret prep work done before today. Now he wanted to be as far away as possible until the raid was completed, but he knew this would only momentarily shield him from what would follow since he had agreed to testify if called upon to do so. And that was almost a certainty.

Ace didn't feel good as he drank another beer, but he would have felt a whole lot worse if he had been fully aware of what was happening behind his back and what was to come.

CHAPTER 4

FRIDAY MID AFTERNOON

A car that Ace recognized pulled up in the driveway. Ace instantly recognized the two agents that got out of it. His stomach churned as the doorbell rang.

"May we come in?" Agent Foster asked.

"As if I had a choice," Ace replied and led them into the living room.

"May we speak to you alone?"

"I'm home alone. Jo Ann's gone to grocery store."

"Good."

Ace began to sweat, and his eyes began to dilate. At first, the agents merely stared at him until his hands began to tremble as his heartbeat increased as he began to breathe harder. Finally, Agent Douglas spoke.

"Our deal's going to be modified," he told Ace in a flat even voice. "How that will happen is still up in the air."

"You screwed over us. You were told to keep your damned mouth shut."

"I swear I haven't said a word to anyone. What are you talking about? I've done everything you wanted me to."

"Hope you enjoy prison."

"Tell me what's wrong."

"What's wrong is that one of our goals was to confiscate the firm's assets and then determine which ones originated illegally."

"I told you who the custodians are and gave you my passwords to access them. ... And their account numbers."

"Didn't do us much good. There was nothing there at either the Kraken Bank in Singapore or the Binance Reliable Bank in Liechtenstein."

"Come on now!"

"Not a farthing or even a nickel."

"But a lot of that money belonged to our other clients."

"I guess it's gone too. I repeat ... there wasn't one red cent either place. It all went into cyberspace moments after we got to your office. The money's zinging somewhere around the planet. Someone had to know we were coming. ... And the only outside person who knew was you. You messed with the bull, boy, and now you're about to get the horn."

"Do you know which computer was used to pull the trigger?"

"Yep! Someone named Jin Woo. He apparently had a fail-safe mechanism in his computer so if he had an emergency all he had to do was push one button to either send everything into outer space or instruct someone else to do it for him."

"But what's going to happen to our other clients' money?"

"I guess they're just up shit creek unless we can unravel this situation."

"But they didn't do anything wrong. What about their securities portfolios?"

"Like I said — G-O-N-E. You deaf or something?"

"But they're going to blame me! Some of these people are my friends."

"Maybe used to be your friends. Like I said — Shit happens. Won't make any difference anyway. Your lying ass is gonna be in jail anyway — for a long time."

"This isn't fair. I swear I didn't tell Jin Woo or anyone else what was going on."

"Life ain't always fair, Mr. Low-Life. You play with fire, you eventually get burned. And if you play with the Feds, you get a permanent vacation at taxpayer expense. When that happens, don't forget to send me a postcard and keep me on your Christmas card list."

CHAPTER 5

LATER THAT FRIDAY

"Jo Ann, we need to talk," Ace said. "We need to do it before Matty gets home and it's still just us here at home."

"Is something wrong?"

"Not something. Everything. I'm in trouble."

"I know you played hooky from work today and took the airboat out. And I saw the windshield on your car."

"That's not what I'm talking about. Midas is done, and I'm in bad trouble."

Ace then told Jo Ann about the FBI raid on his office and how the principals had been arrested for being complicit in a money laundering scheme perpetrated by some of their largest hedge fund clients. It turns out these clients were shell companies for the Chinese Triad."

"And they were laundering drug money? How disgusting. But why didn't you get arrested? You're a partner."

He then told her about his meetings for the past month with the FBI, and how he had avoided being arrested by cooperating in giving them the company records and other information they demanded.

"I swear, honey, I didn't know any of this was going on until the Federal agents told me about it. I had no choice. They told me that unless I cooperated with them that they would name me as an accomplice and I'd be facing the same long prison sentence as the people who committed the crime."

"So you're not going to jail?"

"I don't think so. That's what they promised."

"So you're only out of a job?"

"I think so."

"What's going to happen to the money your clients invested with you?"

"They should be OK. The investments are still there."

"One of those is my father's bank. Your firm was, in effect, his trust department. People from all over Wakulla County trusted their money to him because they respected and relied on him, and he trusted you."

"I know, sweetheart. What can I say? I'd say I'm sorry, and I am, but it wouldn't do any good at this point."

"But we're disgraced. ... And our families are disgraced as well. I'm glad your parents aren't alive to see this. If they were, it'd kill them. They were so proud of you. ... How could you? ... How will Matty face the kids at school."

"That expensive school may be out the window. Honey, I swear I didn't know. We're all victims."

"So what happens now?"

"I honestly don't know."

"For the moment, I'll give you the benefit of the doubt. ... But you better not be lying."

CHAPTER 6

5 PM FRIDAY

The now too familiar black FBI car turned into Ace's driveway. Ace went out to meet them instead of inviting them into the house so they could talk alone. After speaking to them briefly, he felt flushed and faint like he was about to have a heart attack. As he walked back in a daze, he tripped over a crack in the sidewalk and almost fell down. By the time he opened the front door he was trembling.

"Honey, what I'm about to tell you is about to be one of the hardest things I've ever had to tell anyone for my whole life."

"What now? How could things possibly get worse? You better not have been lying to me before. About the only think positive I can think of lately is that we still have a roof over our heads."

"I'm afraid that won't be for long."

"You've got to be kidding me. I thought you said you had a deal."

"But now they're accusing me of not living up to it, and the FBI modified it. Midas Insights was using two off shore banking custodians — one in Singapore and one in Liechtenstein — to hold the clients' assets. Well, the day of the FBI raid someone folded both of those custodians, cleared all the assets out of both banks, and swept them into cyberspace. The computer instruction was put in through Jin Woo's computer. The Feds are accusing me giving him a heads up. Believe me when I say I didn't do it. I was in Coopertown that day out on the airboat. I'd never be stupid enough to try to cross the FBI anyway, even if I hadn't been out there."

"And they can't trace their assets?"

"A mechanism was set up to bounce the assets from one place to another all over the globe. The FBI doesn't know where they ended up. Apparently there was a fail-safe mechanism set up ahead of time in case a worst case scenario ever took place, so it was a matter of just hitting a button to instantaneously start the procedure."

"You are talking about the Triad's assets, aren't you?"

"No, everyone's. They cleaned both custodian banks out one hundred percent."

"So, all my dad's bank's clients are cleaned out?"

"Every penny."

"My folks will have to leave town. Everyone in town will blame them. They'll never live this down. ... So does this mean that you're *now* going to jail?"

"No. The Feds didn't renege on that part of our deal. But they are confiscating all of our assets that came as a result of my employment with Midas."

"But *that's* ... basically everything we own. Our home and everything in it. We bought all of those things after you went to work for them. And even one of our cars is leased by them. ... And your salary pays the car note on the other one. ... And you're out of a job! ... And no CPA firm is going to hire you! ... And ... and ... and ... what client will ever trust you? ... We're so screwed."

"We still have a few assets they can't touch. My inheritance — which is dad's house, car, and boat in Crawfordville. And ... at least they're not sending me to jail."

"Might as well be. Crawfordville might as well be a jail. That's what it's going to be. How will I ever be able to face the people there after all their savings, which were their futures, have gone up in smoke? Don't forget I grew up there."

"I know, honey. I did too."

"And how am I going to face my folks day after day knowing *you* ruined my dad's bank?"

"I didn't do it. The Triad did."

"So what? Their money's still gone — and their future along with it. And what about Matty? He's just a kid."

"At least we'll have a roof over our heads that's paid for, and I can take up fishing if I have to. And you *can* get a job. I know fishing. I helped dad for many a year. We'll just have to take it one day at a time. I know it won't be easy.

"I promise you I didn't try to play games with the Fed. Please believe me and stick by me. I love you and Matty more than anything in the world. We need to have a family meeting when Matty gets back from the movies."

"Yes, we do. And I'm going to let you run it. I'm not going to try to explain your mess to him. You made it; you explain it."

CHAPTER 7

TWO HOURS LATER

Matty came in gushing over the latest James Bond flick and headed for the refrigerator to get a cold drink.

"Son, before you go to your room, we need to have a family meeting."

"Sure. What's up, dad?"

"Pull up a kitchen stool, Matty. Sometimes life isn't fair just because you expect it to be. You think it's supposed to be fair which is why we have these expectations. But in reality, life is random. It's not vacuum packed. Through no fault of your own, it can be tough and cruel at times."

"What are you trying to say, Dad? Have I done something wrong?"

"No, son you haven't, but our family is facing a challenge. But it's one we'll overcome together. Hard times will always pass since nothing lasts forever. I want you to remember no matter how bad things seem in the near future, it will literally be impossible for them to remain that way forever. Even if we were to do nothing, our neglect will eventually have an impact on matters ... even if it doesn't necessarily change things for the better immediately. Time will wait for none of us. We may be called upon to temporarily let go of past expectations to deal with what we may have in front of us. We will learn what we can control and what we can't."

Matty just sat there with his mouth open wondering what Ace was going to say next. Jo Ann looked away as she began to silently sob.

"Matty, Dad's business is folding. Some bad people used it to commit crimes, and some of those people are being arrested."

"Are you being arrested?"

"No, son. But I'm out of a job, and the government will be confiscating some of our assets that came as a result of my compensation from the firm.

We'll have no income until I can make new arrangements. We will also have to move, and you'll be going back to the public schools until we get things straightened out."

"Is there anything I can do to help?"

"No, son. Just cooperate with your mother and give her all your support. I'll be leaving in the morning. Let me repeat. I'm counting on you to look after your mom while I'm gone and help her any way she needs you. I'm going up to Crawfordville to put your granddad's house back in order so we can live in it for the time being. You and your mother will stay here in this house until Christmas holidays begin. Won't be long. They're almost here."

"Yeah, dad, they start at the end of next week."

"That's almost no time. Then, you and your mom'll join me up there, and you'll start in the high school there second semester. I'm not exaggerating when I say things are going to be tight for a while, but we'll make it."

"Yes, sir."

"Tell you what, I'll take some Christmas decorations up with me tomorrow, and I'll get us a Christmas tree before you and mom get there. We'll have a nice Christmas despite all this."

Tank, their male boxer, picked that moment to nuzzle him.

"Oh, Tank just reminded me. Why don't I take him with me. That'll be one less thing you'll have to deal with."

"That's fine."

"And one last thing. I'm sure that the fact that Midas' folding is going to make the news. And some of your schoolmates may try to give you a hard time. I don't want either you or your mom to discuss anything with anyone without my permission. That especially goes for the news media. There's nothing you can say that'll make things better. You can only make things worse and maybe jeopardize what I'm working on. And I don't want you telling anybody where I've gone. It's none of their business.

"Does all this work for you? Do we have an clear understanding of what I expect out of you both?"

"Yes, dad. I guess we do."

"Let me repeat. I haven't done anything wrong, but as I said earlier, life isn't always fair. And when it's not fair, we just have to take the cards that are dealt to us and make the best hand that we can out of them. Some people may use my company's demise as a reason to give you a hard time. And they may say some things about me that are untrue. But don't believe them. I am not a criminal. I'm a victim, and you and your mom are as well ."

"Yes, sir."

"And maybe by the time you go back to school the FBI will get things under control, arrest the culprits, and our life can begin to return to normal."

"Oh, and one last thing. Don't tell anyone in Miami where we're going to be living. I may be called upon to testify against some very powerful people. Until then, if I can help it, we don't need any more people in Miami than necessary knowing exactly where we are. Matty, this especially goes for you. Don't tell any of your teachers or fellow students you're going. When you leave for Christmas holidays, you'll just leave. All it could hope to do is compound our problems. And we don't need any more unnecessary complications than we already have. And that includes online chats. We're each going to get a new email address.

"Oh, one last thing. I've asked the FBI to get each of us new cell phone numbers, and they said they'll take care of it. Comprende? Everyone understand? Do you agree, mother?"

CHAPTER 8

Ace had an eight and a half hour drive ahead of him Saturday. Crawfordville was in the panhandle at the other end of Florida, and Florida is a very big state. The bulk of the drive would be on Florida's turnpike, but long is still long. He planned to leave about four in the morning to miss Miami rush hour traffic and hopefully get to Crawfordville after lunch. On Friday night after dinner, he picked up a rental car since his car would soon be confiscated by the FBI. He then went to Publix and bought some staples he would need up once he got there. Considering what all was going on, Ace didn't want to get out in public and risk a public confrontation any more than he had to in case his notoriety preceded him. When he got back to the house, he got out a legal pad and tried to write down the names of all the Midas Insight clients he could think of who lived in the area.

What a mess! he wanted to scream.

He dreaded having to face Jolene Maxwell, his old boss at the Clerk of Court office, but the meeting he dreaded the most was the meeting with his father-in-law. That would be his first priority when he arrived. Hopefully it wouldn't go as bad as he was imagining, but it wasn't going to be pleasant, even though he was "family." Henry Peeples was one of Crawfordville's leading citizens. Henry's own father had started the Paradise Financial Savings Bank. It had been a mainstay in the community that had helped the area weather the great depression of the 1930's. Hank, as he was known around town, had been chosen as volunteer of the year on more than one occasion. He had been the Boy Scout District Chairman. His wife worked as a volunteer at their church's local thrift shop. The bank had bought the community's public Christmas decorations and also subsidized hanging them around town each year. Hank was one of the most trusted people in the county. And now he would be blamed for violating that trust — all because he had trusted his son-in-law.

No! This is not going to be pretty, Ace thought.

And Jolene! It was her job to prudently invest public funds and earn income so as to ultimately reduce her taxpayers' burden.

My God in heaven! What a total fiasco! And me! Everyone's going to be asking what I got out of all this and why am I not in prison after losing their life savings! They'll never believe that Jo Ann and I are victims too.

Ace arrived in Crawfordville in the early afternoon as planned and immediately drove out to his dad's old house on Alligator Point to unload the rental car. He didn't put anything away, just got it unloaded. He made sure his dad's pickup truck was running, then turned in the rental, and got an Uber ride back to the house. Fortunately it was all uneventful since he got lucky enough to deal with strangers. Now it was time to face the music. He headed for Hank and Cindy's house. When he got there, Hank was out in the yard watering some plants.

Hank didn't immediately recognize Ace's dad's truck. Ace took two deep breaths before opening the driver's side door. Hank then recognized him.

"Ace, now this is a pleasant surprise. What are you doing here? Why didn't you call and let us know you were coming? Where's Jo Ann? ... Cindy, ... Ace is here!"

Cindy Peeples came to the door and rushed out to hug and greet him.

"It's just me. Jo Ann and Matty are back in Miami."

"Too bad. Come on in and let me fix you a glass of tea. Is everything all right?"

"Actually, it isn't. There's some bad things happening at the office. That's why I'm here. I need to talk to you both."

They pulled up chairs around the kitchen table. Ace tried to talk, but at first, no words came out. His throat seemed to just lock up. He took two breaths and tried it again.

"The FBI raided Midas' office yesterday and shut it down. Some of our people got arrested."

Cindy grabbed her husband's hand and waited for Ace to continue.

"It turns out that our hedge fund, Alpha Partners', largest clients were shell companies for Chinese gangsters — the Chinese Triad —, and they were using us to launder illegally made monies. They accused some of our principals of being complicit."

"My God!" Hank uttered. "Were they?"

"I don't think so. Please believe me when I say I certainly wasn't aware of any of this."

"Thank heavens that the investors' money was safe and not comingled with anyone else's money and was being held by an independent custodian," Hank said analytically.

"That's not exactly true. That's why I drove up here this morning and didn't just call you. It turns out that unbeknownst to our firm, these clients had shell corporations who owned the custodial banks. One was in Singapore and the other in Liechtenstein. We were using those custodians on very attractive terms at their insistence.

"The firm elected to go along with them because of the custodian banks' relationship with an OTC crypto currency trader that we didn't know was also owned by another one of their shell corporations. This is where most of their deposits originated. Hank, we're talking about billions of dollars here, and without them as a client, Midas would still be a local smalltime money management company. They literally made Midas into what it is today and wouldn't take no for an answer on anything they demanded."

Hank looked like he was about to explode, but Cindy said, "Hank, let Ace finish."

"It turns out that the Triad had a mole in our office who had set up a failsafe mechanism in case it was ever needed. When the FBI raided our office, he put it into play. All of the assets in both custodial banks were immediately swept into cyberspace and then bounced all over the globe. The FBI has no idea where any of them ended up."

"You mean their assets!"

"No, everyone's assets. Nothing was left behind in either custodian bank. They are now an empty shell."

"Just for the hedge fund!"

"No! Every asset in every division of our firm. All of Alpha Partners' monies — all of Security Investors' money — and all of Asset Alliance's money. They all used the same custodians."

"And all my bank's trust funds and my bank customers' investment accounts?"

"And Wakulla County's taxpayer money, the policeman's, the fireman's, and the hospital's retirement accounts as well. They stole it all."

"You're the one who introduced me — and the whole damned county — to these mutha f..."

"Hank, watch your language."

"... people."

"How was I to know? They victimized everyone. And now the government's taking almost all of Jo Ann's and my personal assets as well. And I'm out of a job."

"But you don't have to live here. We do."

"No, sir. That's not the case. Jo Ann and will be living here too. The Federal government's confiscating almost all of our assets, saying that they were bought with money that I was paid by the firm. All we have left that they can't get to is dad's house, boat, and pickup."

"So, what happens next?"

"The firm'll be put in a receivership, and the receivership will send out letters to the clients affected. I came up here today to tell you what's going on so that you can call people as soon as possible instead of waiting for that to happen. I knew you'd feel that you owe people that. It's the right thing to do. I'll help you any way that I'm allowed to. Now I've got to go find Jolene this afternoon and tell her what's happening. I'm not looking forward to it."

"I guess you know she's got an election year coming up."

"Wonderful! That's just peachy! Thanks for giving me a head's up though. Hank, believe me. ... I don't know what to say. I ..."

"Don't say anything else. You've said everything you need to say. Now, if you don't mind. Just leave," Hank said in a low, flat voice as he stared intently at Ace.

Hank's face was expressionless, almost impassive, and his eyes, though vacant, seemed to bore a hole in Ace's brain.

Cindy said nothing. She knew better than to get in the middle of this situation until her husband cooled down.

"And don't call me. I'll call you when I want to meet with you again. I need some time to think."

CHAPTER 9

Ace left his in-laws' home with mixed feelings. On one hand, he was relieved that this meeting had not deteriorated into a shouting, threatening, or name calling confrontation. But Hank's closing statements played over and over in his mind as he drove away.

And that expression!... It was almost like I was dead.... He's never looked at me that way before. I almost wished he had screamed at me.... Or threatened me.... He never cracked a smile or gave me any encouragement that things might ever be right between us again. Reminds me of that time I backed into a post and dented the back bumper on daddy's truck. I kept waiting for him to scream at me, but he just looked a hole through me and said nothing. His eyes said it all. They said, 'You're stupid.' I would have preferred that he had yelled.

And Hank's vacant eyes today made me feel the same way ... almost like I was stupid and dead to him instead of the father of his grandson.

Ace glanced down at the gas gauge on his father's truck. There was less than a quarter of a tank of gas. He figured he'd better fill it up before he tried to track Jolene down and give her the bad news. He went by Phil's Super Duper Mart. They had both gas and the rest of the grocery staples he would need at the house to make the weekend. Also some beer. He had a feeling he was going to want some. He really didn't want to get out again in public more than he had to for the time being.

As Ace filled the truck, a man who seemed to be about his father's age kept looking at him as he filled his own tank. Finally he spoke.

"You're Jigs' and Maggie's boy, aren't you?"

"Yes sir, I am. You look familiar, but your name isn't coming to me. I've been gone from the cape for a while."

"Yeh, you live in Miami, don't you? I'm Steven Hale. I'm a commercial fisherman like your dad was. Your dad really knew his business. He was one of the best."

"That's right. Big Steve. I remember you now. I apologize for my bad memory. Steve Junior was a few grades ahead of me. How's he doing?"

"Junior's doing just fine. He joined the Navy right after high school and ended up in the Special Forces. He was an explosives expert. He did his time honorably, and now he's back here. I'm mighty proud of him."

"What's he doing?"

"... Fishing ... and some salvage diving and demolition, would you believe? Got his own boat. ... You're the investment guru, aren't you?"

"I don't know about guru. I have spent most of my career working for an asset manager."

"I know. Your dad was so proud of you ... and your mom too ... Jigs used to brag, 'My boy's a regular Wall Street wizard.' He always said Jolene Maxwell hated to lose you, but you were destined for bigger things and she didn't want to hold you back. Jigs said his boy was slated to catch big bucks rather than big grouper. Hope you're not like that Gordon Gekko in the movies."

"People like him are only in the movies. We're not as glamorous as all that."

They both laughed.

"And Mr. Peeples down at the bank also said nice things about you. He said that's why his bank was using your firm as an investment advisor and recommended that we do so as well."

"Thank you, sir."

"I followed their advice and invested some money through them with your firm. My family's small potatoes, but that money is awfully important to us. We worked hard for it and caught and sold a lot of fish to get that money together. Now it looks like it's going to be needed. I guess you know my dad died."

"Yes sir. My dad mentioned that to me one time. Fine man," Ace lied.

Since Steve Junior had been older than Ace was, they had never run in the same circles, and he actually knew little of the Hale family.

"Yes, he was. He fished too. Spent his whole life on these waters. Lost him a few years back. Now my mom's up in her eighties. Starting to lose it. Dementia. We've had sitters stay with her in the daytime, but now she needs someone twenty-four seven.... And those sitters are getting harder and harder to find.... And when you do find a good one, you can't afford them. We've either got to let her live with us or put her in a nursing home."

"Sorry to hear that."

"Mama and my wife never always saw eye to eye even when she was right in the head, and it's gotten worse since mama started slipping. So I guess the nursing home's our only option. Thank goodness we've got that investment account.... I was shocked to learn what nursing homes cost nowadays. ... Don't think we could handle it without that money. ... I don't want to burden you with our problems, but I thought you ought to know so when we do start withdrawing some of the funds ..."

"Thank you for telling me, sir. Tell Steve Junior hello for me and tell him I hope he catches lots of fish. I need to go now, but I'm glad I ran into you. I hope everything works out with your mama."

Ace left without buying the grocery items he had planned to buy. He just wanted to get on down the road and away from Steve Hale as soon as he could.

And this is just beginning. And I've only been in town for a few hours. God, I wish we didn't have to move back here.

CHAPTER 10

Ace nervously rang the bell by Jolene Maxwell's front door. Her car was in the driveway so he knew someone was home. Plus, she almost never went into her office on Saturdays. He could hear the television playing inside the house. He knocked. Jolene came to the door.

"Well, this is a surprise," she said. "And what are you doing in town, Mr. Booker?"

"I came up here partially to see you," Ace replied. "Do you have time to talk to me privately?"

"This sounds serious. Ted's playing golf, so it's just the two of us here. Is something wrong? Have you got a medical problem? You don't have a family problem, do you?"

"No. I have an employment problem that unfortunately is going to result in a problem for you as well. Let's go in the house so I can tell you about it."

They went in the living room. Ace repeated what he had told his father-in-law.

"Let me be sure I have this right. Not only has Midas Insight been closed down by the FBI, but a hacker has absconded with all the client assets as well?"

"That's correct. And right now the FBI is at a total loss as to where the assets got transferred to. I'm pretty sure Jin Woo, one of our partners and one of the firm's founders, was the person who set things in motion. The transfer instructions originated from his computer, and he had relatives in the Triad that none of us knew about. And obviously the scheme that precipitated the transfer had been set up well in advance and only took

32

seconds to accomplish. This was planned and planned well by someone with a very sophisticated knowledge of technology."

"And let me make sure I've got this right. You didn't know that the custodian banks were controlled by Triad shell companies?"

"I didn't. I can't speak for anyone else in our firm. I guess it'll all come out over time."

"How much did they make off with?"

"Over four billion in investments."

"Weren't you running money for Paradise Savings?'

"Trust funds plus local money that came to us as a result of their referrals."

"Have you talked to Hank yet?"

"Just came from his house. He was not a happy camper."

"I guess not. I'm not either. I guess you know your firm has gone a long way to destroying both my reputation and credibility as well as Hank's."

"We didn't do it knowingly. Our largest clients did. Our reputation, along with the firm, is shot as well."

"There's an old maxim in financial circles — know your customer."

"I guess we didn't know ours as well as we thought we did, and some of our people will probably end up going to prison as a result."

"Is one of those going to be you?"

"No, but I'll be on probation, and if I ever try to leave the state without the court's permission, I'll be sent up to do hard time. Plus, the government's confiscated almost everything Jo Ann and I own."

"So what's next?"

"They're appointing a receivership. I don't know what happens after that. Joleen, ... I'm sorry."

"Heh! ... That's the understatement of the year. Sorry doesn't do a damned thing for me right now. ... Just leave. ... I've got to think what I can do to minimize the damage. Get me the contact numbers of the relevant people I'm going to be dealing with. I've got *your* cell phone number. I'll be calling you. I can't believe I trusted you. I never thought you'd let me down," Jolene said.

Ace could hear the barely disguised disgust in her voice.

"Please believe me when I say I'm not the one who violated your trust. We're both victims. This has destroyed my professional career ... and may end up destroying my marriage and family."

"And my career in public life as well."

CHAPTER 11

LATER THAT FRIDAY

Ace left Jolene's house wondering what unspoken repercussions would soon be coming from both Hank and Jolene. Neither of them were the type to fly off the handle and scream irrational threats, but neither of them were passive people who would wait before going on the offensive — despite Ace being "family" to Hank and almost "family" to the Jolene. And neither of them were people anyone would wanted as enemies. You did not want to get added to their shit-list. Both were determined people who had resources at their disposal and money to back them up.

He passed the Grab and Go and remembered that he still hadn't bought the remaining staples he had intended to in his haste to get away from Steven Hale at the Super Duper Mart. He was relieved when he saw only a pimply-faced clerk and no customers in the store. He got in and out as soon as he could before that could change. He picked up some milk for his raisin bran the next morning, a twelve-pack of beer for today, and a few more items.

Is this what I have to look forward to? Ducking everyone everywhere I go? And shit! The news isn't even out yet.

When he got back to his dad's house, he called Jo Ann to let her know he'd arrived safely. He wasn't prepared for the conversation that followed.

"Honey, I'm here. I'm tired. It was a long drive and seemed even longer since you weren't with me."

"I wish I was there instead of here. It's bedlam here. I've been stalked by news people all day."

"Already?"

"Both Fox Channel 7 and Fox News' weekend Fox and Friends show picked up the story. They've both been running it all morning."

"Oh, shit! I'm sorry, honey."

"And it was in the Sun Sentinel's Saturday edition. I'm sure it'll be in the Herald's combined weekend edition tomorrow. I cancelled my standing tennis date with some of the girls at the club. No telling what Matty's going to be facing at school come Monday."

"All he's got is this week until Christmas holidays …."

"Huh! Easy for you to say. You're not a fourteen year old. You know how vulnerable they are at that age. And how mean other kids can be if they feel they have an advantage."

"I don't know what to say except I'm sorry. I wish I could do something about it."

"Oh, I think you've done enough."

"Sweetheart, don't be like that. I feel bad enough already. I'll make it up to both of you when you get here. I promise. Just do what I said before I left. Stay away from these people. 'No comment.' That's our answer to everything. The FBI's working on it. If anyone has to talk to the press, let it be them. Order a pizza from Domino's and stay in. … I need to go now. I love you."

Ace hung up and began to think.

If Fox in South Florida has picked up on the story already, that means Fox in Panama City probably did as well. And Fox News is a national broadcast.

And USA Today sells papers here — Thank God they don't sell that many.

Damn, damn, damn, damn!

Thank God the Apalachicola Times and Port St. Joe Star are weekly and won't be coming out again until next Thursday. I wonder if Forgotten Coast TV's streaming service will be running the story. But I still have to worry about the Wakulla News and the Wakulla Sun.

One thing's for sure. If the word's not out now, it won't be long.

What … a … damned … mess!

… But I won't have until next Thursday. You know Joleen and Hank have got to start calling their most important people first thing Monday. … If they don't begin to this weekend.

Shit! Shit! Shit! And triple and quadruple shit!

Ace's call with Jo Ann suddenly gave him another frightening thought.

I almost forgot. Midas was running Bowes-Carlson's endowment fund! Poor Matty! He's going to be catching double hell at school.

Ace decided if he were going to get a Christmas tree like he promised Jo Ann and Matty he'd better do it this afternoon while he still had some semblance of anonymity.

They're not exactly giving those things away. And I can't afford to piss money away that we may need.

… And I don't want to run into someone by accident like I did Steven Hale … if I can avoid it.

Maybe I just need to go out in the woods and see if I can find a sand pine to cut down. Then I'll come back here, turn on dad's TV and my iPad and see if Midas is on either of them.

With that thought in mind, he headed out to unlock his dad's storage room to see if his dad had a bow saw and some work gloves. He found both of what he needed and threw them into the back of the pickup along with a piece of rope and a ratty old moving blanket that smelled like mildew.

CHAPTER 12

When Ace went back in the house, the day descended on him like a ton of bricks. It was overdue. The long drive, the come-to-Jesus meetings with Hank and Joleen, his paranoid fears at the Super Duper Mart and the Grab and Go, the talk with his wife, Jo Ann. It was all almost too much for one day. Especially after it had been piled on top of Friday's events in Miami. He felt completely emotionally depleted — as a cumulative buildup of being worn out, exhausted, burned out, wiped out, knackered ... all of the above — took hold. It was too early to go to bed. Turning on Fox News would probably only make him feel worse — if that was possible.

He turned on the TV. DirecTV was still working.

Thank you, God!

He found the smooth jazz channel on Music Choice. He needed something soothing. He went to get a beer out of the fridge but wondered if there was something stronger in the house. He found half a bottle of Jim Beam in a kitchen cabinet.

Good old dad. Still looking after me. Thank you, Dad.

He filled a glass with ice, and then added the bourbon straight. He thought about going out on the patio and listening to the music through the open door but decided against it.

I don't want anyone to know I'm here. Besides that, I feel like these clothes are growing to me. This underwear feels like it's been on for a week. I'll just put on some fresh shorts and stay indoors.

After changing, he settled down on the couch and after about half of the drink he fell into a restless asleep. The Christmas tree would have to wait until Sunday.

Sunday morning the TV woke Ace up since it had been on all night. Jeff Goldblum was playing "Let's Face the Music and Dance" on the piano. Ace had a crick in his neck from sleeping on the couch, but otherwise he felt refreshed — depressed but refreshed. He ate some cereal, took a shower, and got ready to go search for the promised Christmas tree, not bothering to shave. Since he was going into the woods and would probably dirty up his clothes or get pine sap on them, he put on the same ones he had driven up in the day before.

The logical place to search seemed to be the Apalachicola National Forest that dominated rural Wakulla County. It was the largest national forest in the state of Florida, and supposedly it had over 2,500 species of plants. Surely he could find something acceptable there.

The Big Bend Scenic Highway ran through it. Ace took U.S. 98 until it intersected with State Road 65, named the Forest Trail, and then drove into the forest. After some searching, he found a six-foot sand pine, sawed it down, and dragged it back to the truck. He covered it with the moving blanket and tied the whole load down with the piece of rope, only partially obscuring it.

Mission accomplished.

Just as he exited the forest, he met a sheriff's deputy's car going in the opposite direction. After they passed, the deputy turned around and began to follow him, signaling for him to pull over.

He did. They both got out of their vehicles and walked towards each other. Ace recognized him.

Tubby Butler! I'll be damned.

They had never been friends, but Ace was pretty sure the deputy would recognize him. Tubby was a junior when Ace was a senior.

Torrence "Tubby" Butler got his name from the fact that there was never a time when he was skin and bone or lithe and light on his feet. Whereas many people outgrew their baby fat, Tubby never did. Despite being a big dude, six foot two, Tubby was never especially athletic. This was not surprising since every member of his family, including his mom and dad, had been overweight. His siblings had had weight issues as well. In high school he didn't date. When he was a teenager, all many girls who met him for the first time saw was his bulk and would edge away like they were expecting him to have body odor. This caused him to stop caring about the way he dressed and made him want to eat anything that made him feel good.

In his off hours, he retreated into a world of video games, in which he played the handsomest, most muscular character that he could be conceive.

Most of Tubby's family seemed to relish being big and often told truthful your-mamas-so-fat jokes. He had never seriously tried to lose weight until he was an adult since he was considered one skinniest people in his family. Being big was a way of life for him. That's just the way it was.

He had finally partially succeeded in the nineties at the insistence of his doctor with the help of Fen-Phen. After Fen-Phen was removed from the market and he started to bulk up again, he had had lap surgery.

Tubby didn't recognize him at first since Ace had a baseball cap on.

"Sir, may ... ?"

"Tubby, it's me, Ace Booker," Ace said as he took his cap off. "How are things with you? So, you're a deputy now? Have you lost weight?"

"Yes. ... And I go by Torrence mostly now, but I can't seem to shake the name Tubby with people I went to school with so I answer to either. Don't worry. I don't get offended when people call me Tubby. Going on eight years, and I'm keeping the weight off.

"My dad helped get me on with the sheriff's department. I like it.

"So, how's things with you? I married Doris Townsend. She's also working for the in the office of the department. We have a little girl. How about you?" Tubby asked.

"Oh, nothing special going on in my life. Married Jo Ann Peeples, and we have a teenage son. Just making a living," Ace replied.

"You became an accountant, didn't you?"

"Yep, but now I'm the comptroller for an asset management firm."

Then Ace ground his teeth and thought, *You shouldn't have said that, dumbass! Please, Lord! Don't let him ask me which one.*

"So, what's that in the back of your truck?"

"A Christmas tree. The family'll be up here next week."

"Did you cut it down in the national forest?"

"Yeh, I guess I did. They'll never miss one tree. They've got over half a million acres of them."

"Did you get a permit?"

"Didn't know I needed one, and besides that, it's a Sunday. Everything's closed."

"Ace, they're pretty strict about that. You can get up to a five thousand dollar fine and up to six months in jail for illegally cutting down a tree. You're lucky that it's me that stopped you and not a forest ranger ... and that I've known you as long as I have. I'll let you slide this time since you didn't know what the rules are, but ..."

"Now that I know, it won't happen again. I promise. I can't just put it back up out in the forest to start growing again. ... And it'd be a shame for it to just go to waste."

"OK this time but consider yourself warned. Good seeing you again."

"Good seeing you too. And tell Doris hello for me when you get home."

They shook hands and parted ways.

Dodged another bullet. No, not one bullet, two. Glad he's not a newshound and didn't ask me what asset management firm I work for. He wouldn't have been so generous if he'd known we managed the sheriff's department's pension fund.

But you can bet your booties, he won't be in the dark for long since the shit's getting ready to hit the fan before the upcoming week's out.

Damn it to hell, why'd his wife have to be working there too?

CHAPTER 13

When Ace returned to the house, he dragged his illegally harvested Christmas tree behind into the back yard and propped it up in a bucket of water.

Damn it! One thing I forgot to bring from Miami was our Christmas tree stand.

He thought he remembered that his dad had had one and went to see if it might still be in his storage room. It was hanging from a metal shelf bracket high on the wall. It was partially rusty and the eye bolts were frozen in place, but with a little of his dad's WD-40 he was able to loosen them up.

He suddenly remembered that there was a Miami Dolphin game on today and decided to check and see what the score was. It turned out to be a close game, and soon Ace got involved watching it. The Christmas tree could wait. After all the family wouldn't be up until next weekend.

At the game's conclusion, Ace went back out to the storage room to look for an extension cord. The only one he could find looked pretty bad so he figured to be on the safe side. He'd better go buy a new one. St. Joe Ace Hardware used to open on Sundays. Probably still was he began to think:

All I need to do is burn the house down. Then where would we live?

OK, Ace?

Ace to Ace. Ace to Ace.

Scotty, beam me over to Ace, the helpful hardware 'guy.'

I still think 'the helpful hardware man sounds better, but what do I know? After all, the world thinks I'm not the sharpest tool in the shed, just another hoe. And maybe they're right — Midas Triad's hoe.

Enough of this self-pity shit. Let's git 'er done. Hopefully, I won't run into anyone I know.

As Ace left, he saw a sign in the yard a little piece down. The homeowners were putting in a new sidewalk and driveway. It looked like from the materials he saw on the side that both were going to be made of colorful Chattahoochee river, exposed aggregate rock. Since the water table is as high as it is near the coast and therefore unstable, this form of construction was often used if the homeowner could afford the extra cost. It was stronger than concrete and had less of a tendency to crack. And when it did, it cracked less and disguised those cracks better. Some decorative pavers were going to be used as an attractive border.

ANOTHER QUALITY JOB
BY A TO BRICK BUILDING

The company name rang a bell. Then he remembered.
Oh, shit! Midas had their profit sharing plan too. Glad it's Sunday.

****

Ace began his day Monday checking out Fox News and Fox Business to see if they were still running the Midas story. Fortunately, they seemed to have moved on. It wasn't on the local news out of Apalachicola or Panama City either. He began to think:

I guess I'm safe until there's some new development. Then we'll be right back on their radar screen. At least I have until Thursday before the local papers come out. But, oh brother, after that …

Ace then spent Monday doing things around the house. He made sure that all the sheets and towels were fresh. He vacuumed. He cleaned out any questionable out-of-date food items. The grass needed cutting. He checked out his dad's boat. After all, he didn't want the family to walk into a disaster when they came up from Miami. Things were bad enough already. All he needed was a big fight with Jo Ann and to have Matty sulking around the house. Besides, it took his mind off of Hank and Joleen and what they were calling and telling people now that the work week had resumed. He hadn't heard a peep out of either one of them since he had met with them on Saturday. He wondered what the next shoe to drop would be.

After lunch, Ace was exhausted and decided to take a nap. When he woke up and walked outside, he tripped over a paver that had obviously bounced of his front door. Now the door didn't line up right and was therefore hard to close. On top of that a hinge was loose. There was also a dent in the pickup's driver's side door and another paver laid on the ground. Another one had knocked his mailbox partially off its post. They all matched the pavers being installed down the street.

I better nip this in the bud before it gets worse. All I need is for this asshole to hit either Jo Ann or Matty with a brick.

He got in his truck and rode down to the job site. A single brick mason was working on digging out the foundation and leveling it so he could put down the outlining forms on what would soon be the new driveway and sidewalk.

"Excuse me. These look like the same pavers that you're getting ready to put down. I found a couple of ones down at my house exactly like the ones you'll be installing. I don't guess you know how they got there. Are you missing any?"

"Don't look at me, Mac. I ain't been near your damned house. I don't even know which one it is."

"I'm not accusing you, but someone threw one at my house and another one at my truck and a third one at my mailbox. I just thought I'd tell you in case you might have an idea who would do such a thing, and also to tell you that I've reported the incident to the sheriff's department, and they'll be close patrolling my house for the foreseeable future." Ace lied.

"If you happen to find out who the vandal was, I'd appreciate you helping us clear this matter up."

"Probably some kid. Thought it would be funny. There's some pretty crappy ones around here."

"Well, I don't think it's funny at all. ... And they won't either when I give their parents a bill for the damages."

"Yeh, sure, Mac. Gotta get back to work now."

"Nice meeting you. They call me Ace. What did you say your name was?"

"I didn't."

"Well, nice meeting you anyway. By the way, you're doing a really good job. You're very good at what you do. I'm sure the homeowner's going to be very pleased with the final outcome."

"Yeh, I know."

Ace got in his truck, drove away shaking his head and thinking.

Is this the beginning of what I have to look forward to? And the news isn't even widespread yet.... But this is a small community.... And people do talk.... What you wanna bet that Hank's already called A to Brick's owner and told him their profit sharing plan has disappeared and nobody knows where the hell it is? Man o man! What's going to happen when everyone knows?

CHAPTER 14

Ace didn't have long to wait until the question he had posed to himself about A to Brick seemed to be answered. He purposely continued to lie low at the house Monday. He found overdue maintenance jobs to keep himself busy that didn't require him to go back to the hardware store before he had to. The bushes and hedges around the perimeter of the house and yard had become overgrown since his father's death, and he decided to trim them back and put the cuttings out for the trash man to pick up. He trimmed some hibiscuses and put the cuttings out by the road. Then as he trimmed the hedge, an A to Brick truck passed his house, pulled up in front of the trash cans, and stopped to watch him work. The two men in the truck pointed at him, watched him, and seemed to be discussing him. When he looked over, the driver spit on the ground, backed up enough to knock over the trash cans, and then drove away. Later that morning as he was taking a break in a lawn chair, another A to Brick truck came by and once again paused with the window down. The driver glared at him and blew some snot out of his nose. When Ace looked back, the driver threw his Big Gulp container and a candy bar wrapper on the ground.

That's rude and was definitely done on purpose. And right in front of me. He saw me sitting here, Ace thought as he gritted his teeth.

He rose and walked towards the street. The driver gave him the finger as he lit a cigarette and threw the empty pack on the ground. He then drove off. Similar things occurred off and on for the rest of the day. Each time it was an A to Brick truck. He got the message. One thing was for sure. The pavers that had been thrown at his front door and truck and had knocked his mailbox cattywampus had not been an accident or the work of some hooligan teenagers.

Things were about to get worse. Ace didn't have to wait until Thursday to find out what the local newspapers were going to say about Midas. Both the Wakulla News and the Wakulla Sun ran special online editions on Tuesday in which they interviewed both Hank Peeples and Jolene Maxwell. Both quantified the possible monetary impact of Midas' bankruptcy on their institutions. Hank had not revealed which of Paradise Financial Savings Bank's customers were affected, but the resourceful reporters at both papers had identified many of the major ones and had managed to interview several of them. The affected peoples' reactions varied from disbelief to outright anger, and in every case, Ace was identified as the local Midas connection. The Port St. Joe Star also inferred that this was a shame since the Bookers were an old local family who had resided in Crawfordville for several generations and who had used their neighbors' trust to take advantage of them..

So much for waiting until Thursday. My honeymoon's over. — Like I ever had one. I guess it's time for me to start telling my side of the story even though no one's going to believe me, Ace sighed.

He thought about talking directly to the reporters but decided against it. If he said something that either the FBI or any attorneys didn't like and it got published, he could just be making things worse for himself. He'd be better off defending himself on a case by case basis as he had to deal with various individuals.

I've just got to keep the story simple. Number one is that I didn't know what was going on, and number two is that I'm a victim just like they are. Number three will be that it's just a matter of time until the FBI takes control of the situation and makes things right. I'll just keep repeating those facts over and over again and not let myself get dragged into providing unnecessary and maybe conflicting details.

Ace didn't have long to wait until the next incident occurred. It happened when the mailman didn't stop at his house. He just put a notice in the mailbox and kept on going. The notice said that his mail was being discontinued until his mailbox was brought up to code.

He waited until he saw the mail truck coming back in the other direction and signaled him to stop. When the driver did, Ace asked for his mail. The mailman rudely shoved it in his hand. Ace tried to explain to him that some vandals had damaged his mailbox.

"Not my problem, Mr. Booker. This will be the last mail you'll get until the mailbox is repaired. In the meantime, you'll simply have to drive in to the post office and pick it up, but I won't get back down there with it each day until about the time the post office closes. Have a nice day."

He drove away.

"I don't know this guy, but he sure knew my name. ... And now the harassment begins. ... And the post office wasn't even one of the businesses affected. The mailman's just being a shit for the sake of being a shit because of what he's heard. I wonder how many other people are going to be acting the same way — or even worse," he said, talking out loud to himself.

"I'm pretty tough. I've had to be. But Jo Ann's not a tough as I am. She's not used to being snubbed and crapped on. And Matty's going through that teenage phase where he's still trying to find himself and is extremely sensitive about pretty much everything. This ain't gonna be fun."

After lunch, Ace went down to the hardware store to buy some shims and long screws to try to get the front door to hang right again.

When he walked in, the store wasn't very busy, and a clerk he didn't know was straightening some paint cans on a shelf.

"Excuse me, sir. I'm looking for some shims and also some long flathead screws. Would you mind telling me where I can find them?"

"I'm busy. You'll have to find them yourself."

Yes, you are. Busy with busy work. But, OK, Ace. Don't get pissed. Just go find them yourself.

He found the aisle with the screws and began to look for what he needed. Just for the hell of it, he peeked around the end of the aisle. The clerk who was too busy to help him was reading a magazine at the cash register.

Yessiree, you're busy all right. Busy being a dickhead.

After searching and searching, he finally found the shims. They weren't even in the store. They were in a bin back next to the lumber. He got a package and walked back through the store.

"Just for your information, in case someone else comes in looking for shims, they're out back with the lumber. I guess you're new."

"I'm not new. I knew that. Cash or credit card?"

You know, living here's going to be more fun than being shut up in a barrel full of monkeys with diarrhea.

CHAPTER 15

Ace didn't have to wait until Thursday before his patience was tested again. As he drank a cup of coffee and stared out the front window, an A to Brick truck partially sheltered by a tree pulled over and stopped with engine continuing to run. The driver got out, and Ace could see it was the brick mason who was working down the street. The man got a paper bag out of the open bed of his truck. As Ace stood there watching, he looked around to make sure he was alone and walked into the front yard far enough to fling weighted paper bag at Ace's truck that was parked in the front yard. Ace could hear rocks weighting down the bag clunking as it landed in the bed of his truck.

What in the holy hell is going on now …?

He went back into the kitchen to put his still partially filled coffee cup back on the counter. By the time he got back, the truck was driving away.

Can't blame that on some rowdy, hoodlum kids this time. I saw who threw that bag. And caught the sorry SOB red-handed.

He put on some shoes and a t-shirt and walked out the front door to see just what it was the guy had thrown. The moment he opened the door a noxious smell hit him in the face. The putrid, unpleasant odor almost made him dizzy. He saw that a second bag had been thrown while he was in the house, and his front entry porch emanated with a sour, ammonia-like smell that reminded him of rotting meat. A fish head with milky eyes seemed to be staring deadpan at him. Entrails were splattered across the front stoop and onto the front of the house.

He gagged as he walked out to his truck and looked into the truck bed. Another rancid smell caused him to momentarily look in the other direction until he could catch his breath. He could see gills and the slimy entrails of a yellowtail tuna. The cloudy, glossy eyes of the same fish stared back at him. It seemed everything had blueish or a greyish tint to it. The paper bag had only partially broken and still contained part of its contents.

Ace clenched his fist and thought, *It's gotta be about A to Brick's profit sharing plan. Mr. Tradesman, you're not going to get away with this crap this time. I didn't take your money. The Chinese Triad did. ... And turned my family's life upside down in the process. You're not the one who the government took everything away from. And you're not the one who is out of a job and probably unhirable. ... And who will probably lose his professional license. And you're not the one who's living on probation and can't even leave the damned state to look for work. You're not the one who's child has been jerked out of his school in mid-year and forced to leave all his friends behind and move to a new city. ... And whose marriage might end up in trouble as a result of all this.*

Oh, no. You wouldn't know anything about any of that. And wouldn't listen or care even if you did know. You're just an ignorant damned redneck who's striking out the only way you know how. Well, guess what, buster? I caught your sorry ass, and I'm not going to take it lying down.

He shook his fist at the empty street.

"You hear me?" he said to the no longer present workman.

Ace went out into the storage room and found a plastic mop bucket there and a garden trowel. He put on some gloves and scooped as many of the rotten fish entrails into the bucket as he could. He didn't bother to try to hose anything down. He'd do that when he returned. He got his car keys and put the smelly mess into the back of the truck.

Ace drove down to the house where the brawny man was working. The man was leaning against a tree, taking a break, drinking a Red Bull, and smoking a cigarette. His radio was blasting modern country music, and he was facing in the opposite direction so he didn't hear Ace drive up as he waited for the wet Chattahoochee surface to dry so he could wind up this part of the job.

Without saying a word, Ace walked into the yard and pitched the contents of the bucket into the middle of wet Chattahoochee. When the burly workman smelled the rancid odor, he turned and saw the head of the yellowfin tuna staring back at him from the very middle of the driveway.

Brown bloodlines, fish skeletons, and guts had just ruined his newly finished surface.

"I thought you might want this back," Ace said and began walking away with his back to the man.

After a few steps, the brick mason had caught up to him. He spun Ace around and came at him with a roundhouse punch. Ace deflected it with the now empty bucket.

From seemingly nowhere, the man suddenly produced a knife. He thrust it back and forth with wide jerky slashes, causing Ace to jump back each time to avoid the blade.

Ace swung the bucket again, almost knocking the knife from his hands.

The workman staggered backwards but recovered his balance and came at Ace again after picking up the knife.

It was Ace who stumbled this time after his heel got caught in a clump of grass, but his stumble saved him since the knife whizzed by only inches in front of where he would have been.

Ace accidentally dropped the bucket, and the heavy-set workman stumbled over it.

Now Ace saw red. All fear evaporated as adrenaline took charge. He kicked the man in his left knee and staggered him again.

The hulking man was now in pain but still swung stiff-armed both of his two hammy open palms from the outside in at Ace's ears. Ace threw up his forearms like an offensive lineman blocking a defensive back and then charged.

The brawny man tried to slip to the side as his knee failed and, while off balance, tried to an uppercut. Ace slammed his elbow down and away in a downward chop and then caught him square in the face with a punch. Blood spurted from the man's nose, gushing all over the place.

Ace was now out of control. He continued to pound the injured man, over and over, pummeling him unmercifully. At this point, he later realized that he had been so out of control that he could have killed the man and felt no regrets.

Ace charged and head-butted the man in his chest. He then reached up and caught the man's head, grabbing his hair, and rolled him to the ground. The middle of the man's back came down on the blade of a shovel, breaking the handle. Ace thought he heard his ribs and back crack. Still holding his hair, Ace began to beat his adversary's head against the steel shovel blade.

The man grunted and threw up on himself before going limp.

The next thing Ace knew was that he was shoved roughly off the unconscious workman's chest by another person. It was the postman. He had stopped and run into the yard when he saw what was going on. He didn't know who was the good guy or who was the bad guy, but he knew someone had to intervene.

The next thing Ace remembered was seeing the flashing lights from a sheriff's deputy's car. Tubby Butler came running across the yard, ordering Ace not to move. Tubby recognized the brick mason, who was starting to come around and pulled him into an upright position on the ground.

"Max, are you OK?"

"Do I look OK, you fat retard? This shyster conman attacked me. I want him arrested," Max said through bloody lips as the blood from his nose continued to flow down on his work shirt.

"ARREST ME! BULLSHIT! OVER MY ASS YOU WILL! THIS SORRY SON OF A BITCH STARTED THIS SHIT!"

"I decide who gets arrested after I figure out what's going on."

He tried to help Max stand, but Max's knee gave out, and he collapsed again, this time face down.

Max groaned after he hit the ground, "My ribs! My back!"

He continued to scream in agony. The deputy tried to turn him over.

"I think something's broken," Max screamed. "Don't touch me."

Tubby called for paramedics. He looked out at the road just in time to see the mailman, using the confusion to try to get away and finish his route before someone could detain him.

"Shit," Tubby said in frustration, but he knew who the mailman was so he'd just have to go find him later and take his statement.

The paramedics arrived and put Max on a stretcher. As they were wheeling him towards their vehicle, Max looked at Ace and said, "This isn't finished by a long shot. You ain't seen the last of me, Mr. Conman."

After the paramedics drove away, the deputy said, "You just can't seem to stay out of trouble, can you? You've been back up here for less than a week, and I've now had to deal with you twice. OK, let me hear your side of this story, and it better be good, or your ass is gonna get booked for assault and battery — just for starters."

Ace began telling Butler how on the previous day someone had thrown pavers at his house, pickup, and mailbox and how the pavers had matched the ones being used on this job site.

"I came down here and asked Max ... I didn't know his name then ... what he might know about it, and all he did was deny any knowledge of what I was talking about. Then he got huffy with me and told me that it was probably some hoodlum teenagers out doing malicious things.

"Well, this morning rancid fish guts got thrown on my truck and my front stoop, and I saw him do it from my living room window. Walk over here and look at my truck if you don't believe me."

They didn't have to walk that far. The odor verified Ace's account of the events.

"And you ought to see the front of my house. If you don't believe me, drive me down there and you can see for yourself. It's still a mess. ... Anyway, I got a plastic bucket out of my storage room, loaded it with what guts I could scoop up and then drove over here. I told him I was returning what was rightfully his and threw them into the middle of the wet driveway."

"Not real smart," the deputy said.

"I know that now, but I was pissed. I turned to go back to my truck, but he took a swing at me, and I managed to block it. Then he pulled a knife and tried to cut me. Cut me, hell. That white trash SOB was trying to kill me. ... Look! ... Here it is on the ground. ... That's his, not mine. I was able to disarm him with the bucket, but he wouldn't let it be. ... So I beat the ever-loving shit out him until the mailman stopped me. That's when you came into the picture."

The deputy sighed.

"You called him Max. You know who he is?"

"Booker, you've just made yourself a dangerous enemy. He's part of the Pogue family."

"So what? Who're they?"

"The Pogues are probably about the most dangerous rednecks In this whole county. They're clannish as hell. And vindictive. And they stick together. And they never forget their enemies. They're known to get revenge. And they fight dirty."

"Wonderful."

"And I almost forgot to mention. ... There's plenty of them. There's two brothers, Ralph and Herman. Ralph and Herman fish — Pogue Brothers Aquaculture. Call their big boat The Scales.

"Ralph has three boys — Max is one of them. His brothers are Randy and Billy III. Billy's the baby. Call him Billy III since he was the third child. Herman has two boys, Joshua ... they call him Josh ... and Noah, and two girls, Grace Angela and Faith Alice. Noah and Faith Alice are twins. Oh, and both of the girls are kind of radical."

"What do you mean, radical?"

"Well, Grace Angela is a follower of Dutch Sheets."

"I'm not sure I know who you're talking about."

"Reverend Dutch Sheets of the New Apostolic Reformation Church. They call for an end of the separation of church and state — by violent revolution if necessary. They say that was what was intended by the Bible."

"But that's one of the basic principles this country was founded on. Are they traitors?"

"Not in their eyes. They say their allegiance is to the Kingdom of God, not any government created by man, and that the church should be the only governing body on Earth. Their goal is to accelerate Jesus' return and rule of the world."

"My God in heaven!"

"That's who they answer to. And Faith Alice's married name is Duke. The racist Duke family."

"You don't mean like David Duke do you, the KKK man? Holy shit!"

"Her husband Haskell is one of David's kinfolk. Not sure how. But definitely kin. These are the kind of people the Pogues run with. I'm telling you, these Pogues aren't like most people. They hate everyone with a purple passion who's not like them. And make no bones about it, the sisters are just as mean as their brothers are ... maybe even meaner."

"I do think I remember Ralph now. I'm pretty sure my dad had a run in with him way back when ... something about fishing. I think dad may have hired a black deckhand once upon a time. You remember a man named Tyrone Brown?"

"Sure do. I always liked Tyrone. Good solid person and hard worker. You know he disappeared kind of all of a sudden, didn't you? People said he might have moved to Fort Pierce, but nobody ever knew for sure."

Ace didn't answer him. He was too busy sorting all this out in his mind. He refocused when the deputy continued to speak.

"And if what you say is true about your dad and Ralph, you've got another strike against you if he remembers who your dad was, and I'm sure he does. Oh, and by the way, I know about how your hoity-toity Miami money management firm has laid the wood to lots of people around here and cost them their life's savings. It's a good thing I didn't know that on Sunday, or I wouldn't have let you off so easy."

"Let me set the story straight. My firm didn't screw these people. They were bagged by some very evil, very powerful, highly organized people. And I didn't know what was going on, but I got part of the blame. Why do you think I'm back up here? Because I wanted to? No, it's because I had nowhere else to go after the FBI took virtually everything I own and put me out of work. I had to plead guilty to something I didn't do to stay out of prison, and I can't leave the state of Florida for ten years without the court's permission 'cause I'm on probation. I'm sure my license to practice accounting is being revoked as we speak. Me and my family as big a victims as anyone. I hope you'll tell that to people around town. I didn't take A to Brick's profit sharing plan. A criminal syndicate did. Tell people that if you have to talk about us."

"I don't know if you're lying or not, and I don't care. And a lot of other people will feel the same way. All they know is that their money has disappeared with an outfit that they never would have invested with other than because of you, and that you were somehow involved."

"It's not over yet. The FBI is working real hard to try to locate the missing money and return it to the people who lost it."

"You better damn well hope they do. Otherwise I'd hate to be in your shoes. You've already made one enemy — and a dangerous one at that. You heard Max as he was leaving. This ain't over. And I can tell you from past experience, these people don't forgive, and they don't forget. ... And they play a dirty game that doesn't have any rules except the ones they make. And those aren't legal."

CHAPTER 16

Ace was still cleaning the fish guts off the front stoop Thursday morning when Deputy Butler came by. Ace had gone to Ace Hardware earlier and bought a gallon of Simple Green, a long handled push broom, a new mop bucket, and a stiff scrub brush to try to remove the now hardened residue from both the floor and wall. His old mop bucket was still down the street. He had simply forgotten about it in the previous day's confusion. And it probably stunk to high heaven anyway. He cursed himself for not hosing the whole mess down the day before, but he simply hadn't been in the mood to fool with it after the violent confrontation with Max Pogue.

After going to the hardware store, Ace had run by the Grab and Go. Today was the day that both the Apalachicola Times and the St. Joe Star were scheduled to put out the hard copies of their weekly papers, and he wanted to see what they were saying about him. These editions would get far wider distribution than had the on-line special edition that both papers had put out earlier in the week since they would go out for home delivery and also be on all the newsstands. Now, everyone in the county who didn't live under a rock would be sure to know about Midas' demise and its effect on the citizens of Wakulla County.

Instead of the papers being in their usual place in the newspaper vending machines out in front of the store, today's papers had been brought inside and were piled on the floor next to the cash register. This would not only prevent pilferage but also serve to make them into an impulse purchase. And it appeared that both newspapers had loaded the store up with many more than the usual quantity.

Wonderful. That's just wonderful!

When he picked up a copy of each of the papers, he noticed that not only was the story the headliner on the first page of both, but they had managed to put his picture in each paper as well. The St. Joe Star had his old high school annual picture, but the Apalachicola Times had obtained a picture of Ace and Jo Ann at a fancy Miami fundraiser. Ace was dressed in a tux and Jo Ann in a long formal gown, and each of them had a drink in their hand, making them look like rich socialite sophisticates, the kind of couple that the average person was jealous of and therefore detested.

Oh, brother. That picture's going to go over like a ton of bricks. It looks like we're hot shots living the high life at our clients' expense. Boy, will that give people around here something to talk about! I can hear them now. "Those Bookers think their shit don't stink. Well, they're about to learn."

The pimply-faced kid at the cash register looked at the pictures and then back at Ace.

"Hey mister, that's you! Are you some kind of celebrity or something?"

"Yeh, unfortunately. How much do I owe you?"

Ace paid for the papers and exited the store as quickly as he could. He felt like he could feel the kid's eyes in the back of his head. When he looked back through the front plate glass window, he saw why he felt that way. The kid was still staring at him and apparently had been all his way out. The kid couldn't wait to find out why Ace and Jo Ann were front page news. After that, he'd then have something to tell every customer who came in the store.

Ace waited until he had returned to the house before reading the whole articles. They did not improve his frame of mind or his mood. But then he had some work to do. First, he now had a fresh incentive to clean things up. Then he had to finish decorating his illegally obtained Christmas tree.

Jo Ann and Matty were in route to Crawfordville and would arrive that afternoon. This wasn't supposed to happen until Saturday after Matty finished his last week before Christmas holidays, but Jo Ann had pulled him out of school early. Reporters had been driving her crazy, and Matty's life had been unpleasant at school as well.

It was time to pack up and leave Miami — and both of them thought the sooner the better. As he scrubbed, Ace was thinking that both he and Jo Ann were going to soon find out that things weren't any better on this end since Crawfordville was very much a little village where everyone talked to one another and exchanged gossip and secrets.

But there's not a whole hell of a lot anyone can do about it. It is what it is, he ranted to himself.

Deputy Butler parked his car out on the street, got out, and walked over. "Morning, Ace."

Morning, Tubb ... I mean Torrence."

The deputy stood there watching Ace work for a few seconds before speaking.

"Just thought I'd stop by and tell you that the Pogues say they won't be pressing charges."

"Gimme a damn break! Won't press charges! That's mighty decent of those cracker, white-trash bastards. I'm the one who ought to be bringing charges against them. Does it look like I'm out here for my health and enjoyment cleaning up their shit?"

"I wouldn't think like that if I were you. You need to just let things simmer down and not aggravate them further. I don't think you realize yet the kind of people you've antagonized. These are some of the meanest and most vindictive rednecks in this entire county — or any other county for that matter. These people will kill you if you make them mad enough. They'll also go after your family. And Don't forget. There's a bunch of them, and only one of you."

"By the way, how's that asshole Max with the moran's IQ doing?"

"Not well. His knee's going to have to be replaced. He's got a couple of broken ribs, and he'll need a chiropractor to help get his back right again."

"Couldn't happen to a nicer guy — that shit-hook."

"And he's going to be out of work for who knows how long. He can't do physical labor in the shape he's in, and that's all he's smart enough or knows enough about to do."

"Legally."

"You're right — legally. No comment. But the good news is that when the incident happened he was an A to Brick employee so their group medical is hung paying his doctors' bills. Otherwise, they might try to come after you for the money."

"Good luck on that. The FBI took everything I own, and now I don't even have medical insurance for my own family. By the way, how long you reckon Max worked for A to Brick?"

"I would guess not more than four or five years. Yeh, I'm sure that's right. Max just got out of the can about five years ago. — I guess I forgot to mention he's a convicted felon. About the only job he could get paid worth a shit that didn't require some kind of licensing was working for someone else in construction. Almost beat some other drunken redneck to death over at the High Five one night when he overheard him make a lewd wisecrack about one of the Pogue girls out in the parking lot. Then he came close to shooting the other drunk who was driving the pickup when he put a bullet through the windshield. Just missed the guy."

"So he wouldn't have even had much money in A to Brick's profit sharing plan, and it might not have even been vested."

"The amount or statutes don't make any difference to these people. They don't need much of an excuse when they feel someone's messed with them or crossed them — even if it's by accident.

"I'm telling you, Ace. You need to become invisible with the Pogues. But somehow I don't think it's going to be possible. I know I sound like a broken record, but these people don't forget, and they do get even. Anyway, I need to get back to work now. Have a nice day."

"Riiight! Sure thing! Thanks for coming by and making my day, Deputy Sunshine."

"Oh, one last thing I was about to forget about. The Chattahoochee job wasn't ruined. It had dried enough so that the fish entrails you threw on it stayed more or less on top and they were able to pressure wash it after it dried."

"I don't know if I'm glad or not."

"Believe me. Be glad. That's one less thing for the Pogues not to get pissed at you over. If they had to pay to redo that man's driveway. I hate to think ... And the man who owned the house would have hated you as well. You don't need any more enemies."

"Oh, what's one more enemy? I'm sure I'm going to have bookoodles of them in the near future."

CHAPTER 17

Jo Ann and Matty arrived late that afternoon. He helped her unload her car. She got out and walked around the house to give it a once over and showed Matty which bedroom he'd be using. He went in, closed the door and began to continue to play the game he'd been playing on his iPhone during the trip. She reminded him that he needed to unpack.

"Later, mom."

Jo Ann complimented Ace on the Christmas tree. He didn't say a word on how or where he had obtained it or about the run-in with the sheriff's deputy. They then went and sat at the kitchen table, and she drank a canned Diet Coke.

After about five minutes, Jo Ann said, "I really need to change clothes and then go over and see mom and dad. I'd just a soon get it over with before it gets later. I'm bushed. That's a long drive."

"Tell me about it. I just drove it less than a week ago."

"You want to come with me?"

"Would you mind if I stay here? Both the local weeklies just put out the story on Midas today — on the front page, I might add — with pictures of both of us — and I'd just as soon not have to face your father again before I have to."

"You're going to have to sooner or later. You can't avoid him forever."

"I'd just as soon make it later after things settle down a bit. Do you mind?"

"Suit yourself."

Matty came in the kitchen and headed over to the fridge to get something cold to drink."

"Matty, you want to go over and visit grandma and grandpa with me?"

"Do I have to mom? I'm tired."

"No, I guess not. Regardless, I need to go."

"What do you want to do about supper?" Ace asked.

"Can we get a pizza with everything on it?" Matty asked immediately.

"Works for me, but leave off the little furry fish," Ace said. "OK, by you, my dear? Go by Joe Mama's on the way back and get an extra-large one. And if you'll get a takie-outie pitcher of their homemade sangria to go with it, you wouldn't hurt my feelings. You need any money?"

"No, I've got my debit card."

"Better use it now, before the FBI tries to take that away from us too."

Jo Ann gave him that look at said, *Did you have to say that?*

After visiting her folks, Jo Ann cut back over to Joe Mama's to order their pizza. The parking lot was full, and she parked out next to the road behind an old, rusty pickup that said Pogue Brothers Aquaculture on the door. When she went in, a couple at one of the tables recognized her.

"Jo Ann Peeples! Long time no see. I didn't know you were in town. I read the story about Ace in today's paper. I'm so sorry. I know you and Ace well enough to know it can't be true. I'm sure they'll clear all this up soon."

"The FBI's working on it. Just for the record, Ace didn't do anything wrong. He just got caught in the line of fire. They'll exonerate him soon and nail the real culprits. You'll see."

A woman paying for her takeout pizza overheard the exchange. She immediately paid and left, rushing out. When Jo Ann got her order and went back out to her car, the pickup had already gone. She thought nothing of it and drove on home. When she arrived, Ace came out to help her carry their dinner into the house. Both of Jo Ann's headlights had been smashed.

"Did you have an accident on the highway or back in Miami?" he asked.

"No, far as I know, they were fine when I left to come up here. In fact, I had them on, and I parked out by the road since Joe Mama's parking lot was full. The only thing in front of me was a pickup that said Pogue Brothers on the door and there was nothing in front of it. But the pickup was gone when I got back out. And then I came straight home."

"Did you say Pogue Brothers? Come on in the house. We need to talk about them."

CHAPTER 18

Christmas came and went with no further incidents. The Bookers skipped both the town Christmas boat parade as well as the new year's fireworks display. Something embarrassing might or might not happen, but there was no use in tempting fate by going looking for trouble. Jo Ann did manage to get Matty registered for second semester at Wakulla High School, and the coach even allowed Matty, who had been on the basketball team at Bowes-Carlson, to join the team as a bench-sitter and dress out for games even though the season was well underway. Jo Ann volunteered to help with the PTA, but the principal looked embarrassed and then hemmed and hawed before politely telling her that he appreciated her thoughtfulness but that currently they had all the volunteers they needed. Maybe down the road.

Ace and Jo Ann decided to attend Matty's first game. It was between the Wakulla War Eagles and Marianna High School. Mainly, they wanted to show Matty that they were supporting him, but they also wanted to see how he was adjusting to his new school and to see if they could tell if he had started making friends with the other students.

As they were walking into the gym, Jo Ann smelled the irresistible buttery aroma of the fresh popcorn being sold at the concession stand.

"Doesn't that smell heavenly?" she commented.

"That's for sure," Ace agreed. "I'll get us some."

He stood elbow to elbow with other parents, worked his way up to the front of the line, and bought a big bag for them to share. As he worked his way back towards Jo Ann, a gruff looking bearded man wearing a baseball cap, elbowed the popcorn out of his hands. He didn't stop to apologize.

Jo Ann said, "I saw that. You know, don't you, that guy did that on purpose? And you should have seen the smirk on his face after he did it."

"You sure about that?"

"100%. I couldn't read the front of his cap, but I'm pretty sure whatever it said started with a 'P.' He was just being crappy. But I'm glad you didn't start anything with him."

"You're right. It would've been a no-win deal right out here in front of God and everybody. Tell you what. Let's go find some seats ... preferably ones easy for me to get back out of ... and after the game starts, and there's no one back down here, I'll go back and get us some more popcorn."

Once the game got underway, Ace slipped out. He decided to visit the men's room first while it was probably still empty. He was right. He had the place to himself.

After he relieved his bladder, he began to zip his pants back up, still facing the urinal. Suddenly he felt warm liquid running down the back of his legs. Then he smelled it — urine.

What in the holy hell ...?

He turned enough to look behind him. A man dressed as the War Eagles's mascot was peeing on his leg. The man was a parent who was the team's volunteer mascot that year since his own son was playing on the team.

"Max sends his regards."

Ace didn't hesitate and bother to turn around. He instinctively grabbed the urinal for balance, bent partially over, and kicked back as hard as he could straight into the man's hand that was still holding his peeing member. The man grunted and gasped in pain as Ace's heel connected. It had happened so fast that he had been caught by surprise. The man bounced off a toilet stall door across the room and into the stall itself. Before he could gain his wits back, Ace turned and rushed him and began to swing the toilet stall door on its hinges, pounding it into the man's head. He then grabbed the man's head and slammed it into the top of the ceramic toilet bowl. The shark head came off, and for the first time, Ace was able to identify the now bloody face of his attacker.

"Send my regards back, asshole."

"I'm gonna have you arrested for assault and battery."

"Just try. I dare you. ... You need to watch where you walk. Tile floors can get slippery."

"You don't know who you're fooling with."

"No, you're the one who doesn't know who he's fooling with. I know what you look like now, and next time we meet .. if we meet again ... you won't be so lucky. I'm going to remember your ugly face for a long, long time, Mr. Pogue ... whichever one you are."

Ace slammed the toilet stall door into the man one more time just for emphasis before washing his hands as he prepared to leave to go to the concession stand to buy the popcorn he had promised Jo Ann.

He "accidentally" stepped on the man's fingers on one hand before he turned and made one last remark.

"And if you're thinking about filing a complaint, I'll tell the school board what you were up to and, they'll be looking for a new mascot, which will be the least of your troubles. Nod if you understand."

The man just stared at him hatefully.

Ace crossed the room in his direction again. The man nodded.

Ace kicked the costume head across the room just to make one final point.

When he got back up to the stands with the popcorn, passing and nodding at Deputy Butler on the way, Jo Ann asked, "What took you so long?"

"I needed to use the restroom. Had to wait for someone else to finish."

"I know. I can smell it on you. You need to be more careful. I hope you washed your hands."

"You're right. I do. Thanks for reminding me. And yes, I did. Wanna smell the soap?"

"Don't be disgusting."

CHAPTER 19

After Ace got back up into the stands, another fan needing to relieve himself went into the men's room. He didn't see the shark head on the floor and accidentally kicked it. The War Eagle's wounded mascot was also still on the floor in pain in the stall trying to get the energy to get up and thinking about what to do next. He couldn't return to courtside looking like he did. The whole team as well as the coach would see him and want to know what had happened to him. Then someone would report the incident to security, and he really would have some explaining to do. Things were bad enough without him making things worse. He dreaded telling his father what had happened. Ralph was not known for his understanding nature. And not only would he jump his son's bones for his stupidity and the juvenile way he chose to pee on Ace's leg from behind, but even worse, he'd call him a pussy for losing the fight. But he couldn't hide his injuries forever. He just needed to put the right spin on the story when he told it to his dad.

Why don't I tell dad I was the one taking a leak, and the sorry son of a bitch came up behind me and got me with a cheap shot for no reason while I wasn't looking. Yeah, that story should play. And who's going to call me a liar? And that'll piss dad off worse than anything I can think of. Booker has now attacked not just one of his sons but two. If Dad didn't want to get even before now, I can guarantee you he won't sleep good until he rights this wrong against our family and sends the message that nobody, and I mean nobody, messes with the Pogue family and gets away with it. He'll want to bury that dirtbag. ... And he'll do it too ... even if he has to hire someone to make the hit. In the meantime, whenever I can get back on my feet, maybe I'll go on home and tell the coach I ate something that didn't agree with me and got the shits.

Then he had a second thought.

Dad would probably be proud of me if I took care of this situation myself. And I know just who to call — An Dung.

The fan instantly recognized Randy Pogue and momentarily froze. Then he glanced around to see if the perpetrator was still in the restroom and getting ready to attack him as well. He breathed easier when he didn't see anyone. Then he turned to go find security and returned with Tubby Butler in tow.

Butler ran over to assess the damage and to try to help Randy up. The parent just stood there staring and wondering.

A person's not even safe at a high school basketball game? What's this world coming to? he thought.

"Who did this to you?" Butler asked.

"Just got careless. Wasn't watching what I was doing. I'm OK now."

The deputy then remembered seeing Ace.

"Was Ace Booker in here?"

"Haven't seen him all night. Is he at the game? Help me up. I'm going home. I'm out of the mood for watching basketball, even if Junior is playing."

Tubby went to find Ace after he helped Randy stand and made sure he wasn't wobbly.

"Were you just down in the men's room?"

"Naw. Did go buy some popcorn for me and the missus. Why is there a problem?"

"Somebody just beat the shit out of Randy Pogue. You sure you weren't down there? You and these Pogues seem to have a thing going."

"Nope. I'm sure. Just watching the game with my wife. But I can't say that I'm sorry someone beat up one of them Pogues. Shame they keep getting in hot water."

"One of these days, Ace. One of these days, you're gonna go too far."

"I really don't know what you're talking about, Mr. Deputy."

Randy headed straight for An Dung's house. An Dung's parents had emigrated to America after the Viet Nam war where they resumed their former occupation, fishing. But there was more to An Dung's family than most people realized. They were more than just fishermen. They were also drug smugglers and even trafficked people on occasion. They were low-end soldiers for a Vietnamese gang who had dealings with Chinese Triad. Unlike his parents, An Dung was now fully Americanized.

Randy saw that An Dung's truck was home and pounded on his door.

When An Dung's wife came to the door, he said, "Pardon me, ma'am, but I need to talk to An Dung."

The citizens of Wakulla County, including Wakulla County law enforcement, didn't 't know it but Pogue family's relationship with An Dung's clan went deeper than fishing. The Asian Nam Cam gang that they were secretly affiliated with used Pogue vessels and the Pogue family's knowledge of local waters on occasion for their nefarious activities. What had started out as a mutual interest in fishing had developed into an enterprise that was very rewarding as tax free income to the Pogues.

Since the French Colonial period, the wealthy residents of Saigon, especially in the Chinatown District, had been controlled by Chinese Triad protection-racket gangs. Viet Nam's "Godfather," Truong Van Cam, more commonly known as Nom Cam, for years oversaw a vast criminal network that controlled much of Ho Chi Minh City's fourth district. Nom Cam was eventually convicted of his crimes and executed, but the tentacles of his criminal empire and his affiliations with other criminal organizations continued to reach far beyond Viet Nam.

"My deepest apologies for disturbing you at home, but could I possibly speak to you alone on a business matter?"

An Dung invited Randy in, and Randy rehashed for him the events that had transpired so far concerning Ace Booker.

"Let me summarize. This man's name is Matthew Booker, and until recently he was high up in a large but now defunct investment advisory firm named Midas Insight that was headquartered in Miami. And his firm has lost a lot of money belonging to people in Wakulla County. And now he has seriously injured first your brother Max and now you. And you want me to put you in contact with a professional who will take him out once and for all."

"That is correct."

"I want to learn more about this situation. Do you mind if I get back to you after I have a chance to look into it?"

"Not at all. That is what I would expect. My family and I will forever been in your debt if you help me get rid of this person."

"I'll be in touch."

Two days later Randy's phone rang, and it was An Dung.

"I have done as you asked. I do not wish to discuss the matter on the phone. We need to speak again in some place private."

"How about Island View Park?"

"That will work. Come alone. Two this afternoon?"

"I'll be there."

When they got together at Island View Park, An Dung told Randy that there was much more to Midas Insights demise than he knew, and that it was entangled with the affairs of the Chinese Triad. He explained how the Triad had infiltrated Midas's organization and had been using it for their own purposes until it had been shut down by the FBI. He then explained that the reason the FBI had successfully raided and shut down Midas was because Ace Booker, to save his own skin, had cut a deal with them to provide them with the information they needed and would most likely be called upon to testify when the case came to trial. He then told Randy that the Triad was glad to know Ace's current whereabouts since they had a $100,000 bounty on his head.

"Is the bounty open to anyone? Are you trying to tell me that if I were to take out Ace Booker, I could get the hundred grand?"

"That's exactly what I'm saying, and they'd be forever indebted to you."

"Well, shoot. Scratch my order to hire a hit man. I'll just do the job myself."

"Are you up to it?"

"Hell, yes. Damn right I am. My friend, there's things that you don't know about me and my family … and their connections. … Pal, you're not the only people with connections. … If you get my drift. … And we're not totally strangers to violence when it's necessary. What can go wrong? After all, Ace Booker is just a pissant desk jockey. This will be a layup. Or should I say a permanent laydown for Mr. Booker?"

CHAPTER 20

Ace lugged a sixty pound bag of Quikrete back to his dock. He still had five more to lug after this one. There was a place next to his dock that was starting to erode so he was going to make concrete rip rap out of the bags to solve the problem before it got worse. As he dropped it and turned around to go back for the next one, he heard a familiar but not so welcome voice.

"What you gonna do with that?" Randy Pogue said. "Bury some new victims?"

"No. I thought I'd save it for dickhead trespassers like you. What do you want, Randy? You here for another lesson in manners? I would have thought you have learned a few things after I pounded on your worthless ass at the ballgame. But then I guess some people are just too plain stupid to learn. But, you know, that nasty bruise on the side of your face should serve as a reminder of your last lesson, but I guess your memory is only a nanosecond long."

Ace could tell he was already getting to Randy. Randy had been toying with the filet knife Ace had accidentally left on the fish table next to the dock. Now his fist tightened around the handle until his knuckles turned white, and he jabbed the fish table with it before pointing it in Ace's direction.

"You know these knives are good for fileting more than just fish. They're also good for taking the hide or the scalp off of cheap swindlers with smart mouths. I've been trying to imagine while I've been waiting what you'd look like bald. And what's even more satisfying is imagining what you'll look like dead. But you know what's most satisfying of all. Imagining what that

$100,000 bounty the Triad put on your head is going to look like in *my* pocket."

The two men walked towards each other. Randy reversed his hold on the knife so that the blade pointed downward and raised his arm in a meaningsome manner above his head. Ace glanced over and saw the long-handled hoe that he had sharpened the blade on earlier leaning against the fish table. He had left it out so he could use it to chop back the weeds on the eroded spot that he planned to reinforce with the sacks of Quikrete he had just bought for rip rap.

When they were within a few feet of each other, without saying another word, Ace grabbed the hoe handle and swung it with a roundhouse swing, arcing it downward almost like it was an axe, as hard he could. The recently sharpened blade caught Randy in the neck, severing his carotid artery as it also partially severed his neck from the rest of his body. The hoe's blade was just sharp enough to cut Randy's flesh. It posed virtually no resistance. Randy immediately dropped the fillet knife.

Randy's blood didn't simply gush in a constant flow but pulsated in time with his beating heart. At first the fountain of blood came thick and strong, flowing through his fingers as he desperately grasped the gash in his flesh. It flowed over his hand, the thick fluid being no warmer or cooler than his skin. After a few moments, the pulses became slower and weaker as the blood continued to leave his now rapidly paling body. He continued to hold his hand to the gash, but no matter how much pressure he applied, it still gushed between his fingers and oozed under his hand as it spread over his shirt.

Randy's mouth opened, but only one almost inaudible semi gasp emerged. Ace stood watching as if he couldn't hear his adversary's painful attempt to plead for help. It was as if a silent theater production of little to no importance was progressing. He never moved until Randy was prone and had almost bled out, his red blood mingling with the green yard as it took on an earthy hue. Watching Randy ebb away, outwardly Ace's eyes grew steadily duller as he stared, but internally he felt like his own guts had been ripped away since this was the first time he had ever killed a man. The feeling would stay with him for a long time afterwards.

Ace walked over and nudged Randy with his foot. It was apparent to him that Randy was now indeed dead. Suddenly the ramifications of what he had just done began ping-ponging through his brain, raising question after question and issue after issue.

Who's going to buy my self-defense argument? I'll get arrested. And even if I'm later exonerated, when the Pogue family finds out about what I've just done, there'll be no turning back with them. And my deal with the FBI will get cancelled. They already told me what would happen if I got in any kind of trouble.

I didn't see his truck when I drove up, or he wouldn't have caught me off guard. He must have parked it down the street and walked down here. Thank God for that little favor. I guess it'll just have to stay there, and I'll deny any knowledge of it.

He stared at the body.

First thing is that this has got to go before anyone sees it. Damned good thing you can't see way back here from the street. I guess the only thing to do is put him on the boat and take him out to sea and give him a nautical burial. Thank heavens I only have to drag him a few feet from the dock to the boat.

He suddenly remembered that there were some ninety-five gallon extra-heavy contractor bags, some duct tape, and some polypropylene construction twine in the storage room.

That should do to wrap up the body so I don't get blood all over the boat.

He went to get the materials he would need. Ace put one bag over Randy's head and pulled it down towards his waist and used another one to start as Randy's feet and overlap with the first one when they met in the middle. He took an unrolled bag and rolled it around Randy's waist, using it to go over the top of the first two where they met. Then he wrapped all the bags as tightly as he could around the body and secured them with the duct tape, sparing no tape.

Glad I found two rolls. I may need them both.

After that he finished wrapping the body with the construction twine, running it in both directions, looping one run through the next where they crossed to make sure nothing slipped. He then taped the twine down just to be sure.

I guess this is a good as it's going to get.

Ace started to drag the body towards the boat but then realized that not only might that leave drag marks, but also he might tear the bags. So he propped his handiwork up against the fish table and bent down to try to carry it over his shoulder. He staggered as he stood up.

This son of bitch is heavy!

Ace continued to stagger with his heavy load, thanking the good Lord that he didn't have far to go, but when he got it next to the boat, he tripped over a cleat. The body flopped onto the deck of the boat with a thud. Ace stood there panting and gasping from the exertion.

Uh! Uh! Uh! Geez! I'm glad it didn't go in the water. I'm not sure what I would have done if it had. Then I'd a been so sho' nuff screwed.

It suddenly occurred to him that he'd need to weight the body down with something if he expected it to sink.

Of course, t he Quikcrete!

He had one bag already in the backyard but ran to retrieve one more from his truck. He peered around the house to make sure no one was there before going to get a second one and after lugging it back, went to gather up what was left of the tape and twine.

As Ace picked up a bag of Quikcrete to put it on the boat, he began to doubt his game plan.

I'm not so sure I can attach these sacks to the body securely enough to guarantee that it will stay down, and I damn sure don't want it floating back up. That would be sure recipe for disaster.

He suddenly remembered that he had a couple of cinderblocks next to the storage room.

Those'll be perfect since I can loop the twine through them instead of just over the tops of the cement bags. But is the twine going to hold? And for how long?

He went back in the storage room to see if he could find something better. He found a spool of twenty-two millimeter plastic coated telephone wire.

Perfect! It's small enough so that I can tie a loop in one end and then thread it through a cinderblock and around the body a couple of times and then pull it as tight as I can and coil the other end around wire before tying it off on the cinderblock. That should work. And three cinderblocks — one on each end and one in the middle — ought to do the job.

Damn, I'm glad that neither Jo Ann nor Matty are home. I need to get the hell out of here before they can show up. Or anyone else for that matter — like the postman or God forbid, Tubby Butler.

He grabbed the wire and some needle nosed pliers to use as wire cutters and hauled everything he'd need out to the boat.

The body was already beginning to smell since Randy's bladder and bowels had both emptied.

I need to get the shit out of Dodge and do it right now before rigor mortis sets in.

With that in mind, he ran to retrieve the boat key off its peg so he could crank the boat and head out to sea with his grisly cargo.

Just before he pulled away from the dock while the boat idled, he remembered that he needed to hose the area and the hoe down, retrieve the fillet knife, and put them both someplace where they wouldn't be seen. This only took a minute or two.

It's not perfect, but I'll wash everything down better when I get back. Put it this way. It's better than what it was. Now, let's get the hell out of here before my luck changes.

CHAPTER 21

Even though Ace had never done this before, he knew he needed to go at least three miles out. And deep was good. The deeper the better. Shouldn't be a problem since the average depth of the Gulf was about sixteen hundred feet. From what he had read, he just needed six hundred feet or more to be on the safe side for a sea burial (and legal, as if this was an issue). But technically that was the regulation. He turned on his depth finder.

The body disposal went off without a hitch. There wasn't even one boat on the horizon when he dragged Randy overboard, and he passed no one on the way out or the way back in. Ace hosed down the area one more time when he returned and poured some bleach on the hard surfaces around the fish table and the dock. He then put some bleach in his mop bucket, diluted it with some water, and left the hoe blade down standing in the bucket where nobody would see it. He threw the fillet knife in with it just for good measure before going in the house and running his clothes through the washing machine before taking a shower.

I think I've covered all the bases. Now it's time for a celebratory drink. The rip rap will just have to wait until tomorrow.

He filled a couple of Tervis tumblers full of ice — one to drink out of and one for spare ice — and took a bottle of Jim Beam out on the patio.

Ace had had just enough bourbon to begin to calm his nerves when Jo Ann got home. She had been helping her dad parttime, filling in when he needed her at the bank in the teller cage during the hours Matty was at school. She not only made a little money, but it got her out of the house. She had grown up working in Hank's bank.

"You're starting kind of early, aren't you, sweetheart?"

"Hey, it's five o'clock somewhere. Want to join me? I wouldn't mind a little company."

"Maybe in a little bit. I've got some groceries in the car. Picked 'em up after I left daddy's."

"Why don't you change into something more comfortable, and I'll bring them in for you."

"You don't mind?"

"Not a bit."

After the groceries were put up, Ace fixed Jo Ann a vodka and tonic, and together they waited for Matty to get home after school. Jo Ann noticed that Ace seemed somewhat spacy and moody. She told him how she felt like people were giving her the cold shoulder at the grocery store, but he didn't seem to be paying as much attention to her as usual.

"You sure nothing's wrong?"

"Just thinking about everything that's happened to us recently. I guess it's catching up to me, that's all."

"I know how you feel. I'm probably magnifying peoples' reactions to me in the grocery store as well. Let's plan on going to bed early and trying to get a decent night's sleep."

The next morning Ace went to look to see where Randy had left his pickup. He found it at the job site where he had had his original confrontation with Max. He didn't risk stopping.

Later that morning as he was getting around to resuming the rip rap project, Tubby Butler came walking around the house.

"Morning, Ace. How's things?"

"Same old same old, Tubby. What's new with you? You solve some big case already today?"

"No, but I've had a puzzling dilemma come up. You seen Randy Pogue since y'all had that falling out at the basketball game?"

"No, thank goodness I haven't. He's not my favorite person."

"You sure made that perfectly clear. We got a call from his wife this morning. Seems he didn't come home last night, and he was muttering something about you when he left the house yesterday."

"Not surprised."

And as I was coming down your street I saw his company pickup parked in front of that job site where you and Max had words — and more. I don't guess you'd know anything about that, would you?"

"What would make you think that? Why would I give a damn where his pickup is?"

"Oh, I don't know. It's just you and those Pogues seem to have some bad blood between you. ... And I can only see it getting worse not better."

"Wish I could help you, but if I never see any of those white-trash bastards again, it'll be too soon."

"OK, I guess I'll have to take your word for it, but if you see or hear anything, be sure to let me know."

"You can bet on it."

After he left, Jo Ann came out and asked, "What'd the deputy want?"

"Oh, it seems that white-trash scum-bucket Randy Pogue is MIA. Probably out doing something illegal. I told Tubby I haven't seen hide nor hair of him and don't want to."

"I wish those people would just leave us alone."

"Me too, honey. Me too. I'm not out looking for any trouble."

"If you love me and your son, please don't be."

CHAPTER 22

Deputy Butler's next stop after leaving Ace's house to go visit Ralph Pogue.

"Heard from Randy yet?"

"Not a peep. That's not like him."

"I'll be glad to give you a ride over to pick up his truck and bring it back over here."

"Appreciate that, Tub. We'll need to run by his house and pick up the key from his wife, Jewel. Didn't you say it's parked just down from where that shithead Ace Booker lives? ... And where he assaulted Max. Show me his house while we're out."

"I'll show it to you, but I don't want you going down there and starting any more trouble. You hear me?"

"I hear you, but I'm not promising you that I'm listening. That's all up to that troublemaker. If he wants trouble, he's come to the right place. If it's grief he wants, I'll give him all he can handle — plus some."

"I'm going to pretend I didn't hear you say that. Leave Mr. Booker to me. That's my job."

They rode by Jewel's and got the key. She still hadn't heard from Randy and was pretty worried. Butler and Pogue then rode by Ace's house.

"Slow down. I want to see what the place looks like."

"It's just his old man's house. You know, he inherited it."

Ace was looking out his front window when he saw the deputy's car cruise slowly by his house. He could clearly see who was in the car.

Crap! Tubby and Ralph Pogue together. That can't be good.

76

The following morning, after Jo Ann had left for the bank, Ace once again saw the deputy's car stop out by the street, and the deputy emerge, this time alone.

Again. Gimme a break, Ace thought.

Tubby walked down the driveway and back to the dock where he began walking back and forth, occasionally bending over to see something closer. Ace moved to a different window to watch but decided to stay in the house. He didn't want to go out and accidentally cause Tubby's suspicion level about anything to rise any more than it already had.

And besides that, I don't think he's going to find anything. I think I cleaned up pretty thoroughly behind myself.

After about fifteen minutes, Tubby had satisfied his curiosity and left. Then something clicked in Ace's mind.

The hoe! I cleaned the blade with bleach, but what if there's some blood splatter still on the handle. I understand they've got some pretty sophisticated chemicals that can detect that sort of thing. The hoe's gotta go.

He threw the hoe in the back of his truck and drove around until he passed a new house going up. It had a construction dumpster, and no workmen were present. And it was nowhere near to his neighborhood.

Perfect! Ho! Ho! Ho! Adios, Mr. Hoe. And away you go.

The week quickly flew by, but Randy Pogue still didn't come home. The missing person story ran in both papers on Thursday, and after that, it seemed that his disappearance was all anyone could talk about. Everyone seemed to have his own theory about the matter. Jo Ann said everyone at the bank was discussing it; Matty said the same thing about the kids at school.

The Pogues continued to rack their brains trying to solve the dilemma. Jewel was getting frantic.

There was one person who's opinion would have carried more weight if anyone had known to check — An Dung. When he saw one of the newspaper articles, he knew he had to tell Ralph his suspicions. And he needed to tell him in person, not on the phone.

"Mr. Pogue, may I speak to you in private?"

"Sure. What's up? You can talk in front of Billy here. There's nothing that you can say to me that I don't want him to hear. He's family. You got a job for me?"

"Not a job, but I do have some information that may shed some light on Randy's disappearance."

"And you're just now telling me about it?"

"I apologize, sir. I only learned about his disappearance in this morning's paper. I came over here as quickly as I could afterwards."

"You're forgiven. Now, tell me what you know."

"Thank you for being understanding. It's like this. Randy came to me after his confrontation with Mr. Booker at the basketball game. As you know, I do have some connections that very few people know about — and I want to keep it that way. He wanted me to recommend a professional to him who would even the score not only for him but for your son Max as well. He thought it would please you that he took the initiative to avenge your family's honor.

"I told him I'd look into the matter and get back to him. When we talked again the following day, I told him that my sources were telling me that Booker's former employer in Miami had been performing some services for the Triad and that that was the reason the FBI had shut them down.

"But they were only able to do so because Mr. Booker had cut a deal with them by giving them information that they needed to build a case. He did this to save his own hide and would probably be testifying when the case came to court. We're talking about a lot of money at stake here ... And I mean lots and lots of money. ... More than you and I can ever imagine."

Billy III started to speak but kept quiet after Ralph gave him a stern look.

"So, why didn't they just take care of Mr. Ratfink? That's what they usually do."

"And what they planned to do in his case as well. But then Mr. Ratfink, as you call him, up and disappeared, and they haven't been sure where to find him. ... Until now. ... though I'm sure they'd a found him eventually."

"Get to the point. What does this have to do with the Pogues?"

"Just this. They put a one hundred thousand dollar bounty on Booker's head for whoever killed him. When Randy heard that, he said there wasn't any reason for anyone other than him to collect that money, and you'd be proud of him for having the gumption to do so. So Randy told me to cancel his request for me to find him a professional."

"And Randy went after Ace Booker himself?"

"That's correct, sir. I think that's what happened. I never talked to Randy again after that and didn't know he was missing until the paper this morning.

When I saw his truck was found just down the street from where Booker lives, knowing what I knew, it all began to make sense."

Now Billy III looked like he was about to pop he was so mad. Ralph stared him down and shook his head back and forth, and Billy remained mute.

"I wondered about that too. And you're right. Now it all does hang together. This piece of cow shit has maimed one of my sons. And maybe killed one of my other sons ..."

Billy III could contain himself no longer.

"Daddy, let me take care of this summbitch. That's what they trained me to do in the Navy. I'll gut him."

Ralph thought for a few seconds before replying.

"No, Billy. I'm going to do what Randy should have done, let a professional handle Mr. Booker. We've apparently taken this guy for granted and underestimated him. He's obviously more skilled than we've given him credit for — though I'll admit he may simply have just gotten lucky. Either way, I'm not going to risk the only son I have left. And even if you were to succeed, you'd probably get arrested for murder. ... Nope, it's not worth the risk. If the Triad has budgeted a hundred grand to put this piece of shit in the ground, I see no reason not to let them do it."

"But daddy ..."

"No, Billy. That's final. Let the Triad clean up their own dirty laundry."

Billy knew better than to argue with his father once he had made a decision.

Ralph turned back to An Dung and said, "An Dung, my friend. You've done the right thing, and the Pogue family's not going to forget it. I look forward to many more years of doing business with you once this matter is cleared up. Now do whatever you can to make sure the Triad succeeds."

"You can count on it, sir."

"That's all I can ask."

CHAPTER 23

It started out as a normal day but deteriorated quickly after the house phone rang.

Who could that be? Jo Ann wondered. *Nobody I know knows this number since it's Ace's dad's old phone.*

"Mrs. Booker? This is Mia. I'm Mr. Dailey's secretary over at the high school. He asked me to call you. Can you come over to the school? There's a problem concerning Matty."

"What kind of problem?"

"Mr. Dailey'll go over that with you when you get here."

"I'll be there in fifteen minutes."

"Great. I'll let him know you're on your way."

"Has he been hurt?"

"No, ma'am, he's fine."

"I'm on my way."

Ace was out so Jo Ann just left him a note. When she walked into the principal's office, Matty sat in one chair staring glumly at the floor. In another chair across from him was Tubby Butler. A third chair was empty.

"Mia, will you close the door and see that we're not disturbed," Mr. Dailey told his secretary.

"What's Deputy Butler doing here? What's wrong?"

"Please have a seat, Mrs. Booker, and the deputy will explain. Then he needs to ask Matty some questions. I didn't want him to do it without at least one of Matty's parents being present."

"Mrs. Booker ...," Tubby began.

"Jo Ann. Tubby, we do know each other. I've certainly seen enough of you recently."

"Then, ... Jo Ann ... We got an anonymous phone call that there was some drug activity going on over here at the school, and that Matty was involved. I brought a drug dog over here, and he smelled illegal drugs in Matty's locker."

Jo Ann felt like she was about to explode.

"That is complete crap. My son does not and never has used drugs," she said in a loud voice. Then she growled between clenched teeth, "Who was this person?"

"We haven't been able to identify the caller. All we know is that she's a female and has a southern drawl. But we did find some cocaine rocks and a crack pipe in the top of Matty's locker. I need to talk to Matty about it."

"Matty, do you know anything about this?"

"No, mama. You know I don't do drugs."

Jo Ann turned back to the deputy and asked, "Was it hidden?"

"No, it was sitting right there on the top shelf."

"If my son was dumb enough to bring crack and a crack pipe into the school, don't you think he'd be smart enough to at least try to hide it?"

"You would think so."

"Sounds to me like it was planted there as a dirty trick. Tubby, you know we've been having a few problems in that regard recently."

"I know you have."

She turned to Matty and asked, "Matty, do you keep your locker locked?"

"No, ma'am, I don't."

"So anyone can go in it."

"Yes, ma'am."

Mr. Dailey remained silent throughout this whole exchange.

Jo Ann turned back to the deputy and said, "Has anyone handled any of this since it was discovered?"

"No, it's right where we found it. There was no reason to handle it since it was right there out in the open."

"So, maybe it'll have the fingerprints of the person who put it there still on it. What about the locker?"

"Same."

"And Matty, you're the only person who normally goes in your locker?"

"Yes, ma'am."

"I want you to get your fingerprint person over here right now and see if you can find some other fingerprints."

"I don't know ..."

"Tubby, my dad is a very prominent member of this community, and if you don't do as I'm asking right now, the next phone call is going to be to him and the one after that is going to be to the sheriff. ... Your boss. ... And my dad won't be trying to present this whole thing to him and spinning it in your favor. ... And he does have the ears of the county commissioners as well."

Tubby was starting to sweat.

"And when that's done I want the fingerprint man to take fingerprints off all the lockers near Matty's and compare them to the ones in or on Matty's locker."

"I can't take all these children's fingerprints without their parents' permission. And trust me when I say they're not going to give it."

"You better damn sure find a way to do it, or I swear, Tubby, my family will go after your job. ... And with the influence my dad has in this community, there's a good chance he'll get it. I don't mean to be a hard-ass, but this is my son we're talking about. And I believe him when he says someone set him up."

Principal Dailey spoke up for the first time.

"Stop! Now both of you listen. This is on the verge of getting out of hand. You're both getting too emotional and overcomplicating things. And saying things you may regret you said later. After all, we *do* have cameras in the hall that will probably identify the culprit ... if there *is* a culprit.

"Here's what I'm going to do. Mrs. Booker, I'm not going to suspend or expel Matty yet, but I'm not going to send him back to class either. I want you to take him home for a couple of days while the deputy and I look at the camera footage and see if it tells us just who the responsible party is. Then I'll decide what I'm going to do next. I'll be in touch when I know more about what the truth really is, and when I decide how I'm going to handle it."

By the time she and Matty got home, Ace had returned. She brought him up to date on what had occurred that morning.

"I swear to God. We're snakebit. Think it's those damned Pogues again?"

"Wouldn't surprise me."

Later that afternoon, the Bookers' doorbell rang. Before Jo Ann could find her slippers and get to the door, the impatient person rang the bell again. The bell rang a third time.

"Coming. Hold your horses. Be there in a second."

When she opened the door, before she could even identify her visitor, she heard the word "Bitch!" as she was slapped across the jaw so hard that her jaw felt detached.

It was Faith Alice Pogue Duke, eleventh-grader David's mother.

Jo Ann recovered and charged with her head down and butted Faith Alice in her ribcage just below her breasts. The surprised Faith Alice gasped and then grabbed Jo Ann's hair with one hand and tried to gouge her face with her fingernails with the other one as she tumbled over backwards. Jo Ann's momentum continued to carry her forward, and she landed on top of Faith Alice. She began to pummel Faith Alice with the heel of her closed fists.

By this time Ace had made it to the front door and pulled his wife off of Faith Alice. Faith Alice tried kicking both of them from the ground and dragged herself to her feet. Ace continued to stand in between the two angry women.

"You got my David suspended! You and your husband have been nothing but trouble. And he got kicked off the basketball team — all because of you. Things were fine in this town until you Miami bigshots came up here. I hate you with every bone in my body."

"What do you mean I got David suspended? If David got suspended, it's because David deserved to be suspended."

Faith Alice got up and began retreating back across the yard.

"You're going to regret you were ever born. You know who my brother-in-law is?"

"No, and I don't care."

"You will, bitch. You will."

Tank picked that moment to rush out the door growling. Ace grabbed his collar.

"Get off my property and don't ever come back. If you do, it may be the last time you ever trespass on any property because you'll be dead," Jo Ann screamed in the heat of the moment. "I won't be responsible for what happens to you. The law clearly gives me the right to defend what's mine."

Faith Alice saw the Booker's dog and redoubled her efforts to get back in her truck and then screeched away, screaming threats and curse words the whole time. For the first time, they noticed that her son, young David Duke, had been in the truck all the time watching this whole fiasco.

"What was that all about?" Ace asked.

"I'm pretty sure I know. Let's call Mr. Dailey over at the school to confirm it, but I know what he's going to say. That the cameras showed that David put the crack rocks and crack pipe in Matty's locker."

Dailey immediately came on the phone.

"Mrs. Booker, I apologize for not calling you. The Dukes just left here a little bit ago."

"I know and came straight over to my house madder than hell."

"The camera clearly showed David putting the contraband in Matty's locker. I've suspended him for two weeks, and in order to be readmitted, he'll have to have regular sessions with our counselor until the counsellor decides they are no longer necessary. He also will not be allowed to participate in any organized sports until the counselor gives his ok."

"But isn't he one of your better basketball players?"

"Unfortunately, but that fact can't cause him to be treated any differently than any other student in a matter as grave as this one."

"Just for the record, Mr. Dailey, I find your attitude to be admirable and refreshing. And also to go on the record, she threatened me while she was here. Said something about bringing her brother-in-law into the matter. Do you know who that is? Is he local?"

"I wish he was just another local thug. He's the well-known white supremacist David Duke. That's who her son is named after."

"Wonderful! Just wonderful! You just made a sucking day suck even worse."

"I'm sorry. You can bring Matty back to school in the morning. I apologize for the misunderstanding and inconvenience."

"You know what you can do to make things right? Make sure everyone knows Matty did nothing wrong."

"I'll try to put out any rumors that I hear, but I think the best thing any of us can do right now is just not talk about this whole ugly affair and let it die a natural death. The truth will prevail."

"I hope you're right, Mr. Dailey. I sure hope you're right, and it's not just optimistic thinking."

"Mrs. Booker, if I wasn't inherently an optimist about the future, I wouldn't be teaching children."

****

As she had promised, Faith Alice Duke was not going to let this matter drop. When she got back to her office, she dialed her brother-in-law, David Duke. She described to him the events that had transpired with the Bookers thus far from her perspective and asked for his help.

"I can't come, but I'll send Earl over."

"Thank you."

"No problem. If someone messes with one Duke, they mess with us all."

****

As Jo Ann and Ace were finishing lunch, there was a tap on the back slider. It was Tubby Butler. Ace motioned for Tubby to come on in.

"Just finishing lunch. Want a glass of tea?"

"Thanks. I'll pass."

"What do I owe the honor?"

"Got another complaint filed against y'all. Actually, mostly against Jo Ann."

"Don't tell me. Faith Alice Duke."

"Yep. Assault and battery charge against Jo Ann."

"I'm the one who should be filing a complaint against her," Jo Ann blurted out. "The bitch came over her and attacked me."

"We didn't complain," Ace said, "because we were trying to take your advice and not stir the pot with the Pogues any more than we already have."

"Not the way she's telling it. She says she tried to have a reasonable discussion with your wife, but Jo Ann attacked her instead."

Ace and Jo Ann alternated telling Tubby what had really happened. Tubby just shook his head.

"She says you threatened to kill her, Jo Ann."

"I told her if she came back around here causing trouble, I'd defend my property if necessary. I was in a fit of rage at the time I said it. She was screaming at that moment on how this wasn't over and how she'd get me."

"We didn't try to kill her," Ace added. "In fact, I held the dog back and kept him from attacking her."

"I'm just going to let the matter drop unless she keeps on pushing it. ... But she probably won't. Please, you two. Just stay away from the Pogues. I don't want one of them coming after you with a gun. ... And they'll do it."

"All I can say, Tubby, is that we'll try," Ace said. "That's all I can do."

"Thank you. Y'all have a nice afternoon."

CHAPTER 24

"Trigger" or "TB" Bob Perkins — Bob, not Robert, or Rob, and certainly not Bobby — awoke. He had adopted this professional name because of its neutrality. And it had been changed or modified a few times over the years when it became necessary. Only he knew what his birth name really was, an anglicization of the Turkish surname "Pekin, "and that's the way he planned on keeping things.

Bob checked his watch on the bedside table and decided it was now time for him to get going for the day . He had arrived in Crawfordville the evening before and checked into the Gulf Sands Motel. It was nothing pretentious or special, but nothing special was what he wanted. The Gulf Sands was an aging but still reasonably well maintained, locally-owned, fifties style, one-level motel cooled by individual-room, window-hung air conditioners and had been designed for motorists. A guest entered the room directly from the parking area rather than through a central lobby. Good for anonymity. A convenient parking space was provided for its occupant just outside of the room's sole entrance. The motel was designed to serve mostly business and commercial travelers, but since it was across the street from the beach, it sometimes attracted vacationers on a budget as well. It didn't attract a rowdy crowd since it didn't have a restaurant, bar, or even a swimming pool. The only amenities were the Coke machine, the ice machine, and the snack machine in the outside breezeway down the sidewalk. The room's dated furnishings hadn't been updated for years. Just what Bob was looking for.

Bob's name was not the only thing mysterious about him. His dull olive skin usually had grayish tint but sometimes also had a greenish cast with dominant yellow overtones. Consequently, many colors did not look flattering on him because they just didn't feel right. He had an outdoorsy look, making it look like his skin would feel rough and dry to the touch.

Contrasting with his brown skin, Bob's eyes were blue, but the pupil in his left eye was so large that it appeared black and made it look as though his eyes were different colors. People's first impression of Bob was that he was probably of Greek, Spanish, or Italian linage, but that was not the case. It actually stemmed from the fact that his paternal grandfather had been a black Mediterranean from Turkey, a fact that had made him somewhat secretly uncomfortable all his life. This sometimes had made him overreact if he felt like he might be a discrimination target — even though the slight might have been inadvertent.

The forty-seven-year old Perkins was a person who lived in the everyday with a seldom-violated routine. He got up at a scheduled time and straightened the bed out of habit even though the housemaid would finish making it up later. If he was home, he would have made it up completely. He did this because even if every other thing for the rest of the day screwed up, he would feel he had achieved something since he hadn't left it in disarray.

He did a few pushups and a few sit-ups on the floor. A guy in his business never knew when the edge he needed would come from being in decent physical condition. It wasn't all sitting and waiting with a sniper rifle. And you never knew when a situation might head south and you might have to defend yourself or get the shit out of Dodge.

Now, having warmed up, it was time to go across the street to the beach and do his two-mile morning run.

When he returned, he then took a hot shower and dried off. Then brushed his teeth. Up and down. Back and forth. Gargle, Spit. Repeat.

Now he did a simple grooming, making sure he was clean shaven — no beard, long hair or long sideburns, or mustache, checking one last time to make sure he had eradicated any evidence of sleep. Satisfied, he then donned his nondescript wardrobe consisting of khaki cargo shorts and a purposely plain white t-shirt — no cute imprints or advertising that someone might remember. He grabbed his binoculars, a plain khaki-colored baseball cap, and his aviator sunglasses. The only thing that anyone might notice was the full-tang, green-handled survival knife he wore for protection in a polypropylene sheath on his waist. Now he was ready for the day.

He left the motel in his Ram 150 pickup to look for a diner, preferably a Denny's or an IHOP, or something comparable. He would deemphasize the carbs in favor of protein and hopefully have some fruit or at least a glass of orange juice. He drank his coffee with a little bit of milk but no sugar. He made sure not to engage in any unnecessary conversation with any local. His tip was average. His objective was to remain invisible, something he was very good at since he was an unexceptional-looking middle-aged man who people passed on the street and hardly noticed.

Now it was time to get on with his day. Tardiness would screw up the day's rhythm. He reminded himself that he needed not to lose sight of the reason he was up here.

Planning was always essential. Trigger Bob considered himself a "plotter" instead of a "pantser." A plotter planned his moves. A pantser flew by the seat of his pants. He thought his attention to detail was a big reason why he had survived up until now where as some of his competitors had been flash-in-the-pans who had come and gone ... too often to the big Shangri-la in the sky.

Out of habit, he checked his pickup to see if anything was out of the ordinary even though no one except his Triad contact was supposed to know he was here. Today would be spent acquainting himself with the area. He found the local radio station and turned it on, hoping for some local news and to just begin getting a feel for the place. He then turned on his GPS and did an initial check using Google maps, especially familiarizing himself with the part of Wakulla County where the Booker family lived. He briefly thought about the nice hundred thousand dollar payoff he would get at the successful completion of this job and how good that money would look when added to the balance in his offshore account or maybe he'd buy a new truck.

He was glad that Wah Ching gang member Johnny Chang had given him a head's up that the Triad had put out a contract on Ace Booker.

He hadn't told Bob the reason for the contract, and Bob hadn't asked. A contract was a contract. The reason was above Bob's pay grade.

Of course, Johnny had not brought Bob into the deal simply because of the goodness of his black heart but because he expected Trigger to give him a ten percent finder's fee under the table. Trigger was fine with that. No one in his world did anything for nothing unless maybe you were family … and Trigger was definitely not family.

It felt natural to be back in the saddle again. He admitted to himself that he had been getting kind of bored since he had chosen to go into semi-retirement until chance had presented him with this opportunity. And, after all, ninety grand tax free was ninety grand. Old habits died hard.

The Booker house was on Alligator Point. Alligator Point was an eight-mile-long, sparsely populated beach community situated between the Gulf of Mexico and Alligator Harbor and known to be a fishing haven. When he first saw it, he was surprised that the water had a brownish tint rather than being blue or green and briefly wondered why. He rode out Alligator Drive and then onto Sunset Hideaway where the Bookers lived. He rode past the Booker house all the way to the end of the road and then back again to eyeball the front of the Booker residence. Ace's white Ram 150 truck was parked next to the house.

Looks just like mine. Same model and same color even, Trigger thought.

He was surprised to see a manmade cutout on the side of the house for Booker's dock and boat.

That sucker had to be grandfathered in. No way in hell the Corps of Engineers would never let that be dug out nowadays, he mused.

Trigger saw that a house near the Bookers was having a new driveway and sidewalk being finished. A black F-150 was parked out by the roadside just down from it as he drove back towards the Bookers. He didn't see the owner. He found a place to park near to the Booker's home and decided to walk down the beach and scope things out from the back. He took off his shoes to make himself look like a beachcomber and grabbed a Circle K plastic bag so he could pretend he was a shell hunter.

When he got close to the house he heard a ruckus. Two women were going at each other.

One woman screamed, "Bitch!"

He pulled up his binoculars to see what was going on and ambled over to where he could get a good view of the proceedings. The next thing he knew, one of the women charged the other and headbutted her in the ribs and the two went down swinging.

What in the hell ,,,?

The two swung, kicked, and gouged until a man, he assumed to be one woman's husband, got in between them and broke it up. Then he heard the reasons for the fight as the accusations began to fly back and forth. Then he heard David Duke's name mentioned. He knew that name.

KKK Grand Wizard David Duke? Holy shit! What have I gotten myself into the middle of? This job may not be as uncomplicated as I was led to believe.

About that time, an angry boxer came out and would have possibly mauled one woman if it's owner had not intervened and grabbed its collar. One of the women took off running, screaming profanities and threats the whole way. The next thing he saw was the black F-150 he had seen down the street flying by with the woman driving. She slowed down long enough to let fly another round of profanities.

My God in heaven. You talk about a head case!

And that's the same truck I saw down the street — the one that looks just like mine.

I definitely need to think this whole thing out and learn more before I make any kind of move.

Both of those women seem a couple of sandwiches short of a picnic basket.

I'm assuming the one who stayed behind is Booker's wife. But who in the hell was the other cuckoo one — the one who said she's kin to David Duke?

CHAPTER 25

The headlines in both the *Apalachicola Times* and the *Port St. Joe Star* told the same story on Thursday.

WAR EAGLES UPSET BY BLOUNTSTOWN 58-52
DROPS PORT ST. JOE OUT OF FIRST PLACE
IN SSAC NORTH FLORIDA TITLE CHASE

Both articles pointed out that without their star shooting guard, David Duke III, the War Eagles were never really in the game. Never once did they lead.

The following Thursday the newspapers each ran stories about the War Eagles having lost two more games — this time to Cottondale and Wewahitchka. They also pointed out that there was a likelihood that David Duke would be out for the rest of the season due to an undefined disciplinary matter. Suddenly, the War Eagles were the talk of the town. There had been high hopes that this was going to be a championship team.

While the matter might have been "undefined" in the press, it wasn't on the street. The Pogues and the Dukes made sure that the gossip spin blamed the Bookers for the team's change of fortune. Principal Dailey only said, "no comment," and that it was an internal matter.

Ace and Jo Ann both felt like people were giving them the cold shoulder more than ever every time they went out in public. When Jo Ann called to get a hair appointment, the beautician told her she was booked and asked her to call back. When she went in the following day, the other women were mostly silent while she was having her hair done, but she heard a buzz of resuming conversation from outside the front door after she left. Matty said some of the kids at school were taking it out on him as well, making him moody and depressed. He didn't tell his parents that he had been eating alone each day in the cafeteria since no one wanted to sit next to him. He dropped off of the basketball team after a few practices after he was almost injured by unnecessarily hard balls passed to him during drills by irate teammates. The coach didn't try to persuade him to stay.

Contract assassin Trigger Bob Perkins didn't know what to think. Was this creating an opportunity for him earn the hundred grand, or was the Booker family so much in the limelight that he would be at risk if he tried something?

People began to throw litter on the Booker's lawn as they rode by. Ace simply picked it up, even when he saw who the perpetrator was, and said nothing. He wasn't going to win any public debates. People around town had just found one more reason to despise him and his family. He mentioned the matter to Tubby Butler only to be told that he couldn't be everywhere at once and that litter was not exactly at the top of his agenda.

This will blow over. I've just got to be patient, Ace thought. *Damn it! We did nothing wrong. That white-trash Pogue family and their juvenile delinquent grandson, David Duke, are the blame. But you know what? The shit-ass junior league punk got what was coming to him.*

I sure wish we were free to move, but we can't. It's just not in the cards.

The Shark's fortunes continued to deteriorate. They lost to Holmes County High and Liberty. They were rapidly falling to the cellar of their division.

Trigger Perkins returned to Miami for a few days.

I'll drive back up when things cool off and take care of Booker when he isn't under a microscope.

When he came back, he went over to do recon to assess what had changed since he'd left. Ace's street was littered with large nails, obviously purposely thrown there on purpose. Unknowingly, he picked up several in his tires on his first drive past the Booker residence. He parked down the street and made his usual trek up the beach to Booker's house to assess things from that perspective.

This whole stinking matter's dragging out too much. I've got to go on and get it done before someone beats me to it and I don't get a dime of revenues out of this deal — just expenses.

When he got back to his truck two of his tires were going flat.

"Shit fire! What next!" he yelled out to the empty street.

He pulled up next to Ace's parked truck and looked up the names of towing companies on his cell phone. One in particular caught his attention as being appropriate for the occasion — Yank and Yuck Towing – "WE TOW, YOU GO."

They said they'd send a truck immediately. He then got out of the truck, found a place to sit on the ground across the street as he waited.

When he looked up, he saw a septic tank cleanout truck known as a honey wagon lumbering down the street. It parked just beyond the two trucks. The sign on the side said "Give-A-Crap Plumbers." On the back of the truck was a colorful drawing of Yosemite Sam brandishing two pistols. Beneath Sam, he saw a warning for tailgaters that read, "BACK OFF! WE AIN'T HAULING MILK."

The scruffy, dirty-looking driver got out and looked at both trucks. He seemed confused since they were the same model and same year Ram and both were white.

He thought, *Wonder which one belongs to Booker?*

The driver walked around both trucks, scratching his belly through his torn t-shirt before scratching his sweaty ass-crack as he mulled over his dilemma. Without thinking, he scratched his head as he rubbed his fingers through his greasy hair. Then, just as unconsciously, he smelled his fingers before wiping them off on his front.

He wasn't the only one puzzled. Trigger also wondered what was going on.

Trigger wondered, *Why's he looking at the trucks? Are they in his way? I don't think so.*

Trigger just continued to watch. The driver shrugged his shoulders and made a decision. He connected a hose to a discharge outlet and flipped a switch. He began to pump the truck's sewage contents into Ace's truck. He first filled the cab before turning to the bed.

What in the hell ...?

Before Bob could react, the man began to do the same thing to the cab of Bob's truck.

The air suddenly smelled like rotten eggs because of the hydrogen sulfide in the waste. Some of the putrid liquid was light brownish, but other portions were dark brown and even black. He saw a combination of sewage originating from human excreta, food preparation waste, laundry water and bath water waste, the gooey remnants of toilet paper, and the other waste products from normal living. Floating in it were sticks, bottles, used condoms, sanitary napkins, and rags. Trigger Bob wanted to gag.

Trigger's next thought was to grab his nine millimeter Glock pistol, but it was in the damned truck, so instead he just screamed for the man to stop. The worker looked at Bob, surprised to find someone witnessing what he was doing. As Bob came at him, he pulled a knife out of a sheath on his belt but then thought better of the confrontation after he saw that Bob seemed to be more athletic than he was. Trigger noticed a KKK tattoo on one of the man's arms. Instead, at the last second, the driver jumped back into the honey wagon and took off down the street, still dragging the hose behind him spraying more of the truck's noxious contents indiscriminately as the unmanned hose bounced back and forth as well as up and down. The air was full of mingling, putrid odors. The honey wagon vanished quicker than it had appeared.

Bob could only stand there helplessly looking at his flat tires as he waited for Yank and Yuck's tow truck to arrive.

Give-A-Crap Plumbers? I'm going to remember that name. And I don't know why happened what just happened, but I will get that sorry son of a bitch!

Yessiree, Bob. Count on it.

CHAPTER 26

Perkins hoped he'd be long gone before his presence attracted unwanted attention, and he was lucky that this turned out to be the case. The Bookers had gone out in Jo Ann's car and didn't return home until after the tow truck hauled his maimed pickup away.

As they drove down Crawfordville Highway, the odor almost made the Bookers gag. There was sewage seemingly everywhere — on the street, on the shoulders, on trash cans that the trash can's owner hadn't brought back in yet, on the street signs, coating a trailered boat left too near to the street, nothing seemed to have been spared. The boat's name that was originally AQUAHOLIC now read , A-dirty splat-splat-splat-H-O-L-dirty splat-splat.

"AHOL. Seems appropriate," Ace muttered to himself. Jo Ann just smiled.

When they got to their own house, the Bookers were horrified at the appearance of Ace's truck. It was covered in the stinky, still drying, gooey, sewage. A used condom had somehow threaded itself over the top of the antenna and now pointed skyward like a phallic symbol from hell. A reddish-brown tinted sanitary napkin had landed right in the middle of the drivers' seat. Bags of mulch that Ace had not unloaded from the truck bed were reeking with the overpowering rotten egg odor.

At first, Ace just stood there and stared. Jo Ann remained in her car with the windows rolled up and turned her car's air conditioner up to max. He motioned for her to turn into the driveway and park as close to the house as possible. As they stood together on their front stoop and stared at the devastation before them, Ace finally spoke.

"What you want to bet this is some more of the Pogue family's shit?"

"Literally," Jo Ann replied.

"I can hose down the heaviest of it, but I'm never going to get rid of the odor in the truck without some professional help."

"I agree. A complete detail job is going to be mandatory. Let's go in and see what our options are."

They went in the house and Googled local car detailers and found out they had one of two options — Shinezilla or Splash and Dash.

"This looks like a Shinezilla job to me," Jo Ann commented. "I guess we better get at it out front before Matty gets home from school. I'll help. You wanna hose or rake?"

"Whichever one you don't want to do."

"I really don't want to do either one of them."

"You know what I'm saying. But before we start, I want to call Tubby Butler and get him over here to see this. And after that, if those Pogues want to battle, I'll give them a damned war."

"How?"

"I'm not sure yet, but I'll come up with something as soon as I find out for sure who's responsible."

This turned out to be easier than Ace expected. In his haste to depart, the driver had had some pamphlets on his dashboard blow out of the honey truck's open window. The title was "The Septic System Owner's Guide." There was a box on the back of them for the contact information of the pamphlet distributor. They were clearly rubber stamped "Give-A-Crap Plumbers" and had an address and phone number.

When Tubby arrived, Ace showed him the pamphlet.

He sighed and shook his head as he said "Oh, crap! Why me, God!" under his breath.

"Do you know this company?" Ace asked. "And who owns it?"

"Unfortunately, I do. Haskell Duke."

"Same Dukes? I haven't heard that particular Duke name before."

"I wish I could say I haven't."

****

Trigger Perkins found out the same information that Ace did, but he didn't need a pamphlet to give him his info. He'd been there and seen the truck. His main objective now was he needed to identify the driver.

At this point the reason was irrelevant to him.

This should have been Booker's battle, not mine.

They made a bad mistake, however. They dragged me into it. It may have been accidental, but at this point I couldn't care less. They messed with the bull. ... Now, somebody's fixing to get the horn.

Trigger also found out from the girl in the office at Yank and Yuck Towing what his only two local options as far as vehicle detailers went were. Shinezilla seemed the best option to him as well.

All he could do now was wait, but he vowed as soon as his truck was cleaned and returned, he would pay Give-A-Crap a visit and give *them* some crap this time — a dose of their own medicine.

He didn't know that he and Ace were on the same page since Ace was thinking the same thing.

CHAPTER 27

Trigger Perkins paid extra to get his truck cleaned and waxed as soon as possible. He didn't want to waste any time unnecessarily before going after the culprit. He wanted to do it while he was still madder than hell. He *always* squared things. That's the way things worked in his world — for every action, there was always a reaction. Somebody was going to die or wish he had. Trigger hadn't made up his mind which one yet. And as for Booker, he was on the back burner for the moment.

When Trigger got over to Give-A-Crap, he asked the name of the owner and if the owner might be available. He was told that the owner, Haskell Duke, was not in at the moment, and she didn't know when he'd return. He was usually just in and out.

The only person there all the time was the woman he was talking to.

The same woman I saw at the brouhaha at Booker's house!

He pretended not to recognize her and gave her the best description of he could of the driver, including the driver's tattoo. She told him that they didn't have any employees matching that description, but that the company suspected some teenagers had taken one of their trucks on a joyride earlier in the week. But she said everything had worked out since the truck turned up abandoned and unharmed.

"Miss, the driver I'm looking for definitely was not a teenager."

She just gave him a blank look and shrugged like *so, what am I supposed to do about it.*

"May I have one of your business cards in case I need to talk to you again?" Trigger asked.

"Sure, and if you'll give me one of yours, I'll call you if I learn more."

"Unfortunately, I don't have one. But my name is Jack Jones," Trigger lied.

Trigger left stumped and frustrated, not knowing what to do next.

As soon as he was gone, Faith Alice dialed Earl Duke's cell phone.

"Earl, there was somebody in here asking about you. Said his name is Jack Jones."

It turned out, Trigger's dilemma was accidentally solved the following day when he went to IHOP for breakfast. Sitting at a table in the back corner drinking coffee and eating pancakes was the very man he was looking for.

The song "You Can't Hide" began to play on warp track in his mind as the band sang

You can run, you can't hide
We'll always seek, we'll always find
You can run, you can try
You can run, but you can't hide

He pointed his closed fist at the man like a pistol and pulled the imaginary trigger.

Bang! Got you in my bullseye, summbitch!

Trigger was so pleased at his good fortune he almost couldn't finish his breakfast, but he was a pro so he played it cool.

I'll see what he's driving. Then I'll just follow him and see where he's staying. Then I'll plan my revenge.

He was thrilled to discover that the man was staying at the Gulf Sands Motel, the same motel he was staying in. He waited to see which room the man went into.

121. I'll be damned. He was right down the hall from me the whole time. How convenient!

He noted that the man's truck had a Louisiana tag, meaning the man probably wasn't local. The back of the truck was plastered with bumper stickers, all with the same tone and theme — "WHITE LIVES MATTER," "DON'T RE-NIG IN 2018," "BETTER DEAD THAN RED," and "DO YA FEEL LUCKY TODAY, PUNK?"

When the man left the motel, Trigger followed him to a middle class looking home. The man parked his truck and went up to the front door. A woman answered — the same one he'd talked to at Give-A-Crap Plumbers. He wasn't completely surprised.

"Oh, hi, Earl. Come on in, cuz."

Now I know the jackass's first name, ... Earl. ... And she called him cuz.

The postman came by shortly afterwards and delivered the woman's mail. When Trigger was sure no one was looking, he casually strolled over with an envelope in his hand to make it look like he was putting something into the mailbox and peeked in to see what her name was — Faith Alice Duke.

Holy shit! She's the one that they were talking about before whose husband is kin to the David Duke! And that means he's a Duke too! That explains the radical bumper stickers. This is getting more interesting all the while.

The earworm to the tune "Duke of Earl" began to play over and over in Trigger's brain.

*Duke, Duke, Duke, Duke of Earl, Duke, Duke, Duke,
Duke of Earl, Duke of Earl*

Now he was beginning to understand the unscheduled sewage delivery. They were still getting even with the Bookers.

I guess that's one way of getting in the last word. But kind of a shitty way if you ask me.

He realized he needed to think this situation out before he planned his next move. He sure wish he knew what the two of them were discussing in the house and was curious about what they might be planning as their next move.

If I didn't have a dog in this fight, this might be almost fun to watch, he thought.

As he worked his way back to the Gulf Sands Motel, the earworm hit Trigger again. Now that he was alone back in his truck, he saw no reason not to sing out loud to himself.

*As I walk through this world
Only Trigger can stop the Duke of Earl*

"Damn, son, you missed your calling. You should have been a songwriter. You'd kill 'em then for sure."

He passed a small bar called the Back Door Lounge. It appeared to be a no-frills, gritty, blue-collar establishment. And, best of all, it was open even this time of day and had no vehicles in the parking lot. It seemed to be an ideal place to have a beer with no one bothering or recognizing him, which would give him a chance to think about what he should do next. Perfect.

He got a PBR draft beer from the bar and carried it over to a table by the far wall. As he sipped his PBR, he Googled Earl Duke on his iPhone. Sure enough, there was such a person, and yes, he was one of David Duke's relatives.

Cell phone service seems to be pretty good in here. That's a surprise.

He called Johnny Chang in Miami.

"Johnny? Trigger. I'm up in the Panhandle. Good news is I've located the person you wanted me to find, but the bad news is he's constantly in the news up here and is friends with the law. This turns it into a higher risk situation. But, that being said, I might be able turn that situation into an advantage. Seems like he's started a pissing contest with a longstanding local family who's about as mean as a constipated bear caught in the middle of a briar patch. I've got a question for you to find out. Will I get paid if someone else gets this guy instead of me but if it's because of me? Am I right to say that all they want is for him to be either gone or neutralized? ... Right? ... If so, I think I may have a plan that'll lay off the risk on someone not remotely connected to us and still accomplish the mission's objective."

He paused before speaking again.

"Do I hear you right? Are you asking if I'm willing to work for less? If I can make a no-risk deal out of it, of course. I guess I am.... You'll get back to me? ... I'll be waiting. Thanks, Johnny."

Before he could finish his beer, his phone rang.

"That sure didn't take long. What'd they say? They'll pay half? I can live with that but see if you can get that number up to sixty percent. I do have a cost of doing business. I'll buy you a bottle of booze if you do. Thanks again, Johnny."

He hung up the phone and walked up to the bar to get a fresh beer as he thought.

What you want to bet they're paying the same bounty and the difference is going into chiseling thief Johnny Chang's pocket? I guess there's nothing I can do about that. Shit, it's worth it. 100% of zero is still zero. This way my plan will allow me to get payback on Earl Duke for trashing my truck and still give me a payday for my trouble.

There goes that song again in my head. How about this version, Earl?

David Beckwith

Duke, Duke, Duke of Earl, Duke, Duke, Duke of Earl, Duke,
Duke, Duke of Earl
Duke, Duke, Duke of Earl,
we'll duke, duke, duke it out, duke, duke, duke it out,
duke, duke, duke it out
shit-bag Earl, Earl, Earl, asshole Earl, Earl, Earl,
scumbag Earl, Earl, Earl,
shit-spreader Earl, Earl, Earl
we'll duke, duke, duke it out, Earl, Earl, duke it out, Earl,
Earl, duke it out
Yes, we will, will, will, yes, we will, will, will

My man, Mr. Duke, shit flows both ways. Count on it, pal. And count on
this too. The next time will be my time to be the shit shoveller.

CHAPTER 28

Ace got a call from Shinezilla that his truck was ready and got Jo Ann to run him over to pick it up and pay the bill.

"Boy, it sure looks better than when I dropped it off here, and it smells like a new truck. It didn't smell this good before my accident. You did an excellent job."

"I will admit it was a challenge," Sam Shine, the owner, replied. "It's been a long time since I've seen a vehicle in that bad a shape.... No, let me correct myself ... Actually, I don't think I ever have. And I can't believe I got two of them in the same day ... same model, same year, even the same color ... with the same issues... both flooded with raw sewage. What've got to be the odds of that happening, a zillion to one?"

"You've got to be kidding me? When I got home and found my truck in that condition there wasn't another truck anywhere near there — nasty or otherwise."

"That's because it had already been towed because it had nails in two of the tires."

"Well, I'll be damned. And that truck ended up here?"

"Shore did."

"Do you mind telling me who the owner was?"

"I don't guess it would hurt anything. I didn't know the guy. It was a Florida truck. His tag was from Dade County."

"Another coincidence. Strange. That's where I'm from."

"Let me find his ticket.... Oh, here it is.... A John Perkins."

"Don't know him. You got a number?"

"Yep. 772 563-8837."

"Mind if I tell him you gave me his number and call him? I'd sure love to find out if he might have seen the person who played this dirty trick on the two of us. I wasn't home. I was out with my wife in her car when it happened. This guy just might have seen the perpetrator and will be able to give Tubby Butler the info he needs to find him and make him pay."

"Somebody needs to. I hope he can help. Now, here's your bill."

****

Ace called Trigger Bob's cell phone after lunch.

"H'llo? Who's this?" Trigger replied gruffly.

Very few people had this phone number.

"Sir, my name is Matthew Booker. Are you the person who recently had his truck almost ruined by raw sewage?"

Trigger was momentarily taken aback. How had Booker gotten his phone number?

He's not even supposed to know if I'm in town. What else does he know?

He wasn't sure how to react but decided to play along until he could learn more.

"Mr. Perkins, yes, I had the same thing happen to my truck. Would you mind it if we could get together and try to figure out who did this to both of us? I'll be glad to come to wherever you are so I won't have to inconvenience you any more than I have to."

Trigger did not want Ace knowing where he was staying.

"I don't mind getting together with you, Mr. ... what'd you say your name was?"

"Booker. Matthew Booker."

"Oh, yeah, Booker, but why don't I come to you instead? Where is that? ... How about later this afternoon? Will sometime after three be OK? Mind giving me your address?"

He knew damned good and well where Booker lived.

Trigger drove over to the Booker residence about three-thirty and rang the Booker's doorbell. He had made a decision before he got there that he would dump Faith Alice and Earl Duke in the creek with Ace by positively identifying them. Intensifying their feud could do nothing but help him accomplish both of his missions — fulfilling the contract on Ace and at the same time getting even with the people who had tried to ruin his truck.

Tit for tat. How sweet it would be if I could kill two birds with one stone... . Literally!

When Ace saw what Trigger was driving, he commented on the amazing coincidence that they did have seemingly identical Ram pickups. He then invited Trigger into the house, introduced him to the rest of the family. Jo Ann welcomed him warmly. Matty also politely greeted their visitor and introduced himself.

What a nice family! You seem to meet so few of them nowadays. Almost makes me guilty about what I'm going to have to do to them.... But, hell, business is business.

"Lovely house. I'd love to see more of it," Trigger said. "You mind showing me around?"

Hot damn! Don't get much better than this. I get to case the joint with them showing it to me.

He was looking for anything he could steal later to use to frame the Bookers when he lowered the boom on the Dukes and the Pogues. He made a mental note of a wooden storage block full of knives in the kitchen.

A butcher knife with their fingerprints on it would make a good murder weapon.

Jo Ann joined them and gave him a brief tour.

"I was about to have a beer," Ace said. "Would you join me?"

"Does a one-legged duck swim in a circle?"

Jo Ann got them each a beer and got herself one as well. Matty politely excused himself.

"So," Ace asked as a matter of introductory small talk, "If I might ask, Mr. Perkins, what brings you to Wakulla County?"

Trigger gave Ace and Jo Ann a cock-in-bull story about how he was in the area doing a feasibility study for a South Florida investment group who thought that the Forgotten Coast was possibly one of the last real bargain investment opportunities left in the Florida.

"They could well be right. We have pristine, unspoiled beaches that go from Mexico Beach on the Gulf to St. Marks on Apalachicola Bay. We have great fishing, and we also have Tyndall Air Base over in Panama City."

"By the way, Mr. Perkins, ..." Jo Ann began.

"Please call me Bob.... Mr. Perkins was my daddy."

"... Sure, Uh! Bob.... And we're Ace and Jo Ann.... We're up here from South Florida too. Ace is an accountant, and my daddy is in the financial services industry up here as well. We may know some of the same people. After all, Ace was part of an investment firm there."

Sister, if you only knew the people who know who you are. If you did, you'd be crapping all over yourself.

"No joke?" Trigger replied, feigning surprise, even though he knew their background very well. "Unfortunately, the identities of the people I represent are confidential information."

"So, back to the business at hand," Ace asked, trying to get the conversation back on course. "Did you see who did this to both of us?"

Here we go! Sock it to 'em, Trigger!

"Oh, yes, as a matter of fact, I did. I was stuck on your street with two flat tires when it happened. I not only saw him, but I've also been able to identify him as well.... Though it would be my word against his. The honey truck driver's name was a man named Earl Duke."

"As in being kin to Faith Alice Duke?" Jo Ann blurted out.

"You know the Dukes?"

"Do we know them? We've had nothing but trouble with that family since almost the first day we moved in. Those rednecks are nuts ... dangerous loony tunes.... and meaner than a barrel full of water moccasins," Jo Ann continued, as Ace silently looked at her out of the corner of his eye, wondering if she wasn't saying too much.

She continued. "They're white-trash with a little money."

Sister, how well I know!

Trigger wished he could compliment Ace's wife for her fiery feistiness but kept his mouth shut since he wasn't supposed to know anything about the Dukes. The Aaron Neville song, "Tell It Like It Is," however, briefly did flash through his brain, making him smile.

Instead, he asked with mock sympathy, "If they're as crazy as you say they are, do you have a gun? You might need it to deal with people like that."

Before Ace could stop her, Jo Ann said, "Oh, yes. Ace keeps a pistol in the bar in the den."

"Not that it's any of my business, but I guess I don't have to tell you that you can get in trouble for having an unregistered gun."

"Not a problem. Ace registered it."

Thank you, dear lady. That'll save me from having to try to find that gun. And it's sweet knowing that it's on record of belonging to you. This is getting better and better. My plan to do in everybody on both sides while have them blame each other is looking more feasible all the time.

After staying long enough to make be able to make a graceful exit, Trigger told the Bookers that he hoped what he had told them would prove to be useful and made his departure. When it was all over, Ace invited Trigger to go fishing with him.

CHAPTER 29

As Trigger drove away from the Booker residence, he began thinking how productive his meeting with the Bookers had been and of the ways to possibly frame both parties simultaneously.

"Then I can get out of this backwater hick town and back to Miami where I belong. Maybe I'll drive down to Key Largo to John Pennekamp State Park and go to the beach. No, I've had enough of roughing it. No, maybe I'll go to Sitz Sum. I've never been there before, and I understand they're doing things with food that no one else in town is doing."

But as he continued to drive, he couldn't help but have a conscience attack of sorts. Not over the Pogues or the Dukes.... No way in hell did he feel sorry for them ... He hoped they'd burn in hell with a little help from him ... But for the Bookers.

As bad as I hate to admit it, I enjoyed meeting those folks. They're really pleasant, decent people. That son of theirs is a nice, polite, clean-cut kid. So many teenagers his age are just little shits. They're doing a good job raising him. What you wanna bet he'll grow up to be a very decent adult .... And the parents seem to be a good reliable suburban couple with a good solid marriage. Something I've never known and certainly never had.

For the first time Trigger wondered why the Triad had put a bounty on Ace's head. Then he wondered if maybe getting to know them had been a mistake. He knew he had violated a basic principle of a successful hit man, emotional involvement. He reminded himself that that was why people in his profession should always keep their target at arm's length and as anonymous as possible. His attitude should be no different than it was when he had been an Army sniper. No different than that of the pilot of a bomber flying over an enemy target. They should be nothing more than a faceless bullseye to be hit. Nothing more; nothing less. Hit and go. Out of there. On to the next target. That's the way it should be.

Objectivity. That's the name of the game in my business. These aren't people; they're a contract.

Trigger, don't forget that. If you do, you'll be sorry. Now's not the time to go soft.

Trigger's next tasks were to devise a plan to assassinate Earl Duke using weapons that he would steal from the Booker residence and how he was going to make sure Ace got framed for the crime. Ace may or may not get convicted. He reminded himself that the final outcome was irrelevant. As it should be. The main thing is that Booker would be put out of commission. That seemed to be what the Triad wanted. Otherwise, why did they agree to give him a partial payment if Booker remained alive?

By the time all the issues are cleared up, I'll have collected my money and be out of the picture. Maybe I won't remember what their name was.

Trigger did not feel the same compassion for Earl Duke as he was feeling for the Bookers. Whereas the Bookers had done nothing to offend him, ... in fact their actions had done just the opposite, ... Duke, now that was another matter. First of all, there was the matter of the truck — Trigger always got even when someone disrespected him — even if, as in this case, it may have been accidental. But he had a bigger bone to pick with anyone kin to David Duke. The black Turkish Mediterranean side of him hated racist, white-supremacist assholes of every variety, and the Dukes were one of the world's worst racists and also one of the most vocal racist offenders in the whole United States. He could just imagine what their attitude towards him would be if they knew his lineage.

I'd like to take one of their burning crosses and shove it up their ass.

He briefly thought about burning Faith Alice Duke's house down before deciding to just settle for going after Earl. After all, Earl should be an easier target since was staying at the Gulf Sands Motel.

That should make him an easy mark. We'll take care of him in the privacy of his room, and no one'll be the wiser until the maid cleans up the next day. By then it'll be adios, Trigger Perkins. I'll be halfway back to Miami.

A car horn woke Trigger out of his reverie. He'd been so busy thinking this thing through that the light had changed to green and an impatient motorist behind him was honking for him to start moving again. He started to flip the guy a bird but thought better of it.

I didn't tell Booker that I knew where Duke was staying. Or that that is where I'm staying as well. Yep! That's where I'll bump Duke off and set it up for Booker to take the blame. I just need to break into Booker's house and steal the props I'll need. I'll steal a knife and a gun and then play it by ear on which one I'll actually use.

Sure glad his wife showed me where he keeps his pistol. Not only do I know he has one, but I won't have to tear up the house looking for it. Bet there's a good chance he won't even miss it.

CHAPTER 30

Trigger Perkins was not the only person making plans. Billy III was making plans as well, despite his father's orders that he let a Triad professional handle the Booker matter. Even if he never collected the hundred grand, he wanted the satisfaction of knowing that he, Billy III, a member of the family, had been the one who evened the score. He had no doubt that he had the skills necessary to take out this ex-desk jockey. After all, he'd been in the service. He just had to not get caught doing it. Ultimately he knew when it was all over and he hadn't been apprehended, his dad, Ralph, would agree that he'd done the right thing and appreciate Billy III's true worth and loyalty to the Pogue family.

When all's said and done, it's family ... Don't ever let me forget that.... That's what counts.

Faith Alice had told Billy about the dirty trick Earl had played on Ace, and now he smiled every time he thought about it. He thought about making a similar mess of Ace's boat using fish guts.

Naw! That's already been done.

Besides that he'd have to collect enough fish offal to do the job, and then he'd have to go on Ace's property to spread the "good news."

Shit! That'd end up turning into work. Unnecessary work is something I don't need.

Unnecessary work was not a word the somewhat lazy Billy III was especially fond of.

And it'd stink up his own truck as well. He didn't need to have to take his truck into Shinezilla and risk that Ace would put two and two together and that it might lead Ace back to him.

I don't need that crap and the hassle it'd create.

Neither patience nor cognitive ability had ever been two of Billy III's strong suits. After giving the matter his usual three minutes of concentration and deep thought as he tried to squeeze a sore white-head just above his ass-crack, he decided that while he waited he might as well pick up a little beer money at Ace's expense.

I know just the way to not only frustrate that jerk but cost him some money while I'm at it. I'll raid his crab pots when he's not around. He'll just think his yield his down but won't know why. And then after doing that a few times, I'll snip the ID tags off of some of them and cut 'em loose.... Not all of them at the same time. Just enough to frustrate the hell out of him.... He'll not only lose his catch, but they're not exactly giving new pots away nowadays. Since I have my commercial fishing license, I can sell the crabs and pick up a quick buck or two.

This strategy went well for Billy for a few days, but Ace knew after a day or two that something just wasn't right. It kept happening at about the same place repeatedly. He decided to go out and watch things with his binoculars from his dad's fourteen foot Carolina Skiff. A cluster of mangroves would provide cover. He wore sunglasses under a long-billed fishing cap with a neck flap for anonymity. He soon found out he'd been right as his surveillance paid off. He caught Billy red-handed.

I'll be damned. Another one of those Pogues. Talk about bad pennies that just don't go away? ... Should have known.

Ace pulled out his nine millimeter Walther pistol, cranked his twenty-five horse Yamaha and began inching along the side of the mangroves. He came up behind Billy III as he was leaning over the opposite side of his boat, pushing a just emptied crab pot back in with his gaffing hook.

"How's the fishing today?"

Billy froze. He had been sure he was alone.

"It's illegal to raid another person's crab pots."

"I thought these were mine."

"Bullshit! You lyin' low-life mother! You know better. Or you should."

With no warning, Billy III turned, leaned forward, and, without aiming, threw the gaffing hook like a javelin in Ace's direction as he reached for something on about his waist level. Ace easily deflected it and reflexively, without thinking, squeezed off a shot back. The pistol's unexpected noise surprised them both. The bullet caught Billy in the chest, rocking him backwards onto his back but didn't pitch him out of the boat. He overturned a five gallon paint bucket and blue crabs scurried out of it. A flock of herons, egrets, and bitterns took to the air.

At first, Billy felt an intense burning. He looked down at himself and saw that his chest was a gaping cavity surrounded by a perimeter of abraded tissue that was rapidly filling with blood. As the blood rushed out, he began to choke on it. Ace's bullet had hit a rib and the rib's fragments had begun causing damage to both Billy's heart and one of his lungs. His blood pressure began to drop as the oxygen to his brain shut off.

He vaguely thought that this was not the way things were supposed to work out. He had imagined that the next blood he would see would belong to Ace not him. Neither Ace nor Billy thought about the fact that in a little more than another minute Billy III would most likely be dead. This regret was Billy's last lucid thought before he died.

As soon as Ace realized Billy was gone for good, he began to gather his wits about him. He looked around to make sure there had been no witnesses. Luck had been with him. They were alone except for the birds who had begun settling back down again. He hadn't planned on killing anyone today, but now that it was done, he knew he had to do the same thing he had done with Randy if he planned on staying out of trouble, get rid of the body in the deep ... asap.

Ace tied off to Billy's boat and climbed over the now dead body to retrieve the crab pot that Billy had been trying to shove back into the water, being careful to try to avoid the puddles of spreading blood as he did so. He glanced down to see what Billy had been reaching for.

My God! He had both a gun and a knife. Glad I didn't hesitate. He wouldn't have. Otherwise, I'd be the one lying there instead of him.

He had a brain fart that quickly evolved into a plan. Once he had pulled the crab pot aboard, he then climbed back onto his own boat and towed Billy's until he could tie it off temporarily to a mangrove, retrieving the gaffing hook out of the water along the way.

Ace's next job was to beach his boat and find enough limestone rocks to use to weigh down the crab pot when it had a body attached to it. The twelve ounce railroad spikes he normally used for weight weren't going to be nearly enough.

Now came the most disgusting part of this whole operation, securing the body to the crab pot to ensure that they both sank together. He stabbed the open wound in Billy's chest until the gaffing hook came through his back. Then he reached into the bloody cavity and through the gooey organs and looped the nylon rope back and forth through the whole carcass repeatedly and then through the vinyl-coated steel wire on the pot until he was sure he had everything secured to each other. He almost lost his lunch a couple of times as he did this. He wrapped the cord around and around Billy's neck and pulled it snug with the crab pot as well. The only thing now flopping was Billy's legs, and he wasn't sure what to do about that so he just hit them with a wrench a few times to break them. At the last second, he remembered to take off Billy's shoes and socks so the crabs would be able to get to his feet and ankles to begin eating them sooner.

All this done, he then retrieved the now empty five-gallon paint bucket, dipping it overboard and throwing bucketfuls of seawater throughout the boat to try to dilute the blood before filling one to wash himself off. One last thought was remembering to retrieve both Billy's wallet, car keys, knife, and cell phone. He threw the cell phone in the water immediately. He'd pitch the knife and the keys on the way out as he towed Billy's boat. He'd tear up the contents of the wallet later. All that left was Billy's pistol. He'd save it to blow a hole in Billy's boat to help scuttle it and then he'd pitch it somewhere as well. First things first. The boat could wait. First, he needed to dispose of the body. Then he'd decide where to scuttle the boat.

Now, let's pray I don't meet another boater or an FWC patrol boat on the way out.

Once again, Ace's luck held out and within a couple of hours he was back home showering the remaining blood off of himself and destroying the clothing he had been wearing before Jo Ann or Matty came home.

When Jo Ann came in, Ace announced, "Soon as you change, my dear, I've made us a pitcher of sangria."

"Are we celebrating something?"

"Do we have to be celebrating something? Let's just say we're celebrating a sanguine sangria sunset."

CHAPTER 31

Two days later, as Ace was finishing washing down his boat, he got another visit from Tubby Butler. At first, he just stood and watched Ace roll up the water hose.

"Billy III seems to be missing. I don't reckon you've seen or heard from him."

"Why would I see him? You know what he thinks of me. And if I never hear from him again, it'll be way too soon as far as I'm concerned."

"Oh, I dunno. Just seems like there's been a lot of coincidences and accidents happening with the Pogues recently. And somehow, a lot of them seem somehow to involve you.... Funny! Imagine! Every one of Ralph's children.... And in such a short period of time. What's the odds of that? ... First there was Max."

"He brought what happened to him on himself. I didn't hold him down and tell him to throw fish guts all over my house. He came up with that cockamamie plan all by himself. I just made sure that he knew that there are consequences for acting like a dickhead.... Excuse my French."

"He did pay. And then Randy disappeared."

"No big loss to the world if that scumbag never comes back."

"And then your truck got trashed."

"I'm still trying to figure out who pulled that number. But I've put it behind me. Hell! We both know it was most likely one of those damned stinking Pogues, but I'm letting that one slide. What's done is done, the truck cleaned up."

"I don't disagree that one of them was either involved or maybe hired it done. But I'm glad to hear you say you're letting it slide. But, you know, now there's something mysterious happening with Billy III."

"Hey, you know what they say. If you choose to lie down with dogs, don't complain if you come up with fleas."

"Still.... Awfully strange."

"Ever think that that family's just snakebit? And that it's gotten what it deserved. Shit fire! Billy's a snake in the grass if there ever was one. But even a snake in the grass like him eventually gets his just deserts if he doesn't stay on high alert for his own kind. You know what they say, a snake in the grass is deadlier than a lion in a tree.

"And you expect me to feel sorry for any of them? Huh! No way, Jose.

"So, tell me, is Faith Alice making up shit again? Is that why you're over here bugging me?"

"No, Herman's the one who reported Billy missing. His boat and trailer were found down by the boat ramp at the end of Alligator Point, ... past your house ... but his Carolina Skiff hasn't turned up anywhere since he supposedly took it out fishing."

Ace couldn't help but smile. He hoped Tubby didn't notice.

Fishing, my ass, Ace thought. *You mean crab pot robbing and sabotaging, don't you? Last time he'll be pulling that stunt. The crabs should be making good progress eating him for lunch now. Who knows? I may be harvesting some crabs down the road that fed on him. Wouldn't that be justice?*

"Don't get upset, Ace. I had to ask. After all, it *is* my job."

"I know, Tubby, and I'm sorry if I overreacted. You're right. It is your job. It's just seems like I haven't had a moments piece since the first time I ever laid eyes on that God forsaken family. They've undermined everything we've tried to do. And not just me but Jo Ann and Matty as well."

"Sure seems that way. But I did warn you."

"I know you did. I'll keep you posted if I run across Billy's boat. And if you don't mind, keep me posted as well on your progress at getting to the bottom of things.

"Now, pardon me if I don't weep. I think you of all people should understand why."

Tubby nodded.

"So, unless you got something else, I've got work to do. Thanks for coming by."

CHAPTER 32

Trigger knew he had to wrap things up in Crawfordville before he lost his veil of anonymity. The longer he stayed there the greater the risk that someone would remember his presence. He also reminded himself about objectivity. Objectivity to him was another way of saying professionalism. The successful assassin was the assassin who repressed his feelings and approached his job for what it was — a job.

He knew he possessed a skill that only a few people had, and because of that he was compensated very handsomely for what often required very little actual work. And at a risk factor lower than most people realized. It was all in the planning. Most crimes were crimes of passion against people with whom the killer had had some sort of relationship in the past, thereby setting into motion the pattern that law enforcement used to gain their advantage in apprehending them. In Trigger's case, his victim was normally a complete stranger who in most instances the killer had never met and took place in a locale that was foreign to him. And when the job was completed, usually all he had to do was leave the area permanently with a preplanned exit strategy. It was that simple. He made it a point to refuse to take a second job in a particular area unless an enormous amount of time had elapsed since the initial assignment. And he didn't mean months; he meant years, preferably a decade or more. That's how a guy like him survived, grew old, and retired well fixed.

Corollaries were to never get too difficult or greedy with your employer. Never give them an excuse to send someone else like you after you to even a score or right a perceived wrong. Their good will was imperative. The last rule was always be a man of your word. If you committed yourself to a job, you had to see it through, even if complications or unexpected expenses arose.

I am a man of principles. My principles may not conform to those of mainstream society, but they are my inviable principles, nevertheless.

This job had begun to test both Trigger's patience and principles. It had gotten personal. Not on one front but two of them. First of all, he was beginning to feel empathy for his intended victim. Second, he had singled out a second victim, not for compensation but simply because he couldn't stand the son of a bitch or his family. He could somewhat rationalize his first violation since he had renegotiated his contract so that he could choose to simply neutralize the damage his target could cause his employer instead of killing his victim outright. It would haircut his pay, but he'd still get a nice paycheck. And he wouldn't be burning his bridges with the Triad. He might currently be in semiretirement, but he never knew when he might want to or need to become a fulltime assassin again. But Earl Duke — that racist psycho had to be put in the ground. If for no other reason than to reduce the number of assholes in the world by one.

All of these things were going through Trigger's mind as he drove along. As much fun as he might have by just taking Earl out immediately, he knew he needed to break into the Booker residence and get what he needed to lay the suspicion off of Ace and thereby insure his paycheck. He'd then feel free to "off" Duke and then get the hell out of Dodge and back to his familiar south Florida stomping grounds.

Maybe I'll treat myself to a trip to Cancun.

Trigger began to case Ace's house. He was pretty sure he knew when Jo Ann or Matty weren't there, using her car as a barometer, but Ace was another matter. When his truck was there, he might or might not be home. Sometimes he might leave with Jo Ann, but other times he might be out on his boat, the Aquaholic. He knew if he saw Ace go out, he'd be gone several hours at least. And Matty had regular school hours. Jo Ann, now, that was another matter. She might be gone for hours, but she might just be out on a quick errand like a trip to the grocery store. As boring as surveillance was, he knew it would be best to see both Jo Ann and Ace leave at the same time. The break-in shouldn't take long. He knew what he was looking for, and Jo Ann had shown him where Ace kept his pistol.

It didn't take long for Trigger's opportunity to come. Ace took the boat out, and Jo Ann left at the same time going somewhere. Even if she was just on a short term trip, he was confident he'd be long gone before she returned since he knew what he was looking for and where the items were. Trigger donned some gloves and prepared to break into the Booker household. He had brought some zip-locks to deposit the items in so as not to spoil any fingerprints on them. He was an expert lock picker, but his skills weren't put to the test since the Booker's had left the slider on the back of the house unlocked.

Since he didn't know what he'd use to take out Earl, he wanted both a knife and a gun. He went into the kitchen where he had seen the knife block but decided that they would certainly notice if a knife was missing. He rooted through the drawers until he found an old fillet knife at the back of one that looked like it hadn't been used in a while.

Perfect! And I'm almost positive the fingerprints on it will be his instead of hers.... And it shouldn't be missed.

He carefully put it in the zip-lock. Now it was time to steal a gun. He worried that they would miss gun the Bookers had shown him in the bar. He went through the bedside tables and found nothing. But then God smiled on him again. There was a pistol case in the top of the closet.

Boy, is this my lucky day. I won't steal the case, just the contents and then put the case back exactly where I found it. They'll see the case and just assume the pistol is still in it.

It don't get no better than this. Hallelujah, Trigger! Success! This is flat gonna work! Not that I'm a braggart, but did I ever tell myself how good I am?

Speaking of success and work makes me think of what Vince Lombardi used to say.

"The only place success comes before work is in the dictionary."

Trigger deposited Ace's nine millimeter pistol in another zip-lock and let himself out the unlocked slider again.

As he drove away, he was completely satisfied that he had accomplished his mission one hundred percent and that Earl Duke would soon dead as a dodo bird when phase two of his perfect crime plan was completed. And a payday on the Booker contract would be around the corner.

Yessiree, Bob. Cancun here I come.

Since he was alone, he couldn't resist singing out loud in his truck to the tune of "California here I come."

David Beckwith

Miami and Cancun here I come
Right back where I started from.
Where bowers of flowers bloom in the spring
Each morning at dawning, birdies sing and everything

He smiled as he thought of a Bill Murray saying he'd once heard on SNL. "Whatever you do, always give one hundred percent — unless you're donating blood."

He would soon be donating some blood alright, but it wouldn't be his.

CHAPTER 33

Trigger began to discretely follow Earl Duke to see if his habits helped him formulate a plan of action. He finally tired of tracking Earl. He thought a couple of times that Earl may have picked up on him. He briefly thought about just doing a drive-by shooting to get it over with, but he really did want to leave one of Ace's weapons at the scene to misdirect law enforcement and insure that he was going to get paid by the Triad. After all, he had incurred expenses, and all he got out of bumping off Earl Duke was just personal satisfaction. But satisfaction doesn't spend. The financial payoff would come when he framed Ace Booker and eliminated him as a credible witness against the Triad. And he could always go back and eliminate Ace later if it became necessary to collect his money. It'd be a pain in the ass, but it was doable. Just one more complication in this already snakebit situation.

He finally decided to possibly make the hit at the motel. But before he did, he needed to create some space between him and his victim by checking out of the Gulf Sands where they both were staying and checking in elsewhere. He chose to move to the Econo Lodge. He reasoned he should be able to remain anonymous there until he could finish his business and leave town.

One thing Trigger always prided himself on was his flexibility. The problem of how to make sure the weapon got into the hands of the sheriff's department continued to nag at him. Especially if the hit was forced to happen in a public place.

An unexpected opportunity seemed to come when Earl and Haskell Duke returned to Haskell's seemingly unoccupied office after having lunch together at the Sand Dollar Café. There didn't seem to be a soul around.

Earl Duke is the only one I want, but I'll take two — two for the price of one. Kind of like if you buy one; you get one free.

Since there was seemingly no one else around, he'd just leave the pistol registered in Ace's name and his fingerprints on it in the parking lot for the law to find. No use overcomplicating things. As Trigger targeted in on the two Dukes and began to squeeze the trigger, Haskell reached into his pocket to fish for his door key as Earl reached down to retrieve a package left by the mailman. The door was suddenly opened from the inside, and a familiar head poked out.

Faith Alice!

The bullet missed both Earl and Haskell and caught Faith Alice in the shoulder, propelling her backwards into the office as it went through both bone and cartilage. Earl turned just in time to see Trigger's white Ram pickup speed away from the scene.

As he sped away, Trigger muttered to himself, "Well, you screwed that up royally this time, old man. Not only did you hit the wrong person, but the damned weapon to frame Ace is still sitting right next to you on the seat. Maybe you better just get rid of the cursed thing now. So much for a clean windup to this job in what was supposed to be a nice, easy payday. This job should have been a three-point layup, but it turned into a shit storm instead. Shit! Shit! Shit! And double shit! You're the one who's snakebit! Maybe you should have stayed in retirement."

As Haskell rushed in to help his wife, Earl dialed 911.

Within minutes, both Tubby Butler and the ambulance arrived. As the medics stabilized Faith Alice and loaded her into the ambulance to take her to the hospital, Tubby began to question Earl as to what he had seen. Earl denied having seen the shooter but admitted to seeing a white pickup truck. Haskell went to the George M. Weems Hospital in Apalachicola with the ambulance, and Earl followed as soon as Tubby allowed him to do so. By the time he got there, Faith Alice was already in surgery.

He and Haskell waited for the doctor to come out and talk to them. When he finally did, he told the two Dukes that Faith Alice was stable but in ICU but couldn't have visitors yet. Haskell refused to go home. Earl told him that they needed to talk, and the two men went down to the hospital cafeteria to get a cup of coffee.

"Now, Haskell, don't overreact here and make a scene where people can see us, but I may have screwed up. Before I thought I told Tubby I saw the truck," Earl began. "As far as I'm concerned, this is not a law enforcement matter but a family matter that we need to handle ourselves."

He could almost feel Haskell's blood pressure rising. He was afraid for a moment Haskell would crush the coffee cup.

"I couldn't see the shooter's face, but I saw what he was driving — a white Ram pickup with Florida tags. I know who owns a pickup matching that description."

"Who's that?"

"Ace Booker."

"Let's go get the son of a bitch. He's the one who hurt Max and got my kid expelled from school."

"And may have been involved with Randy and Billy's disappearances as well. The jury is still out on what happened to them. This family seems snakebit recently, and he always seems to be around when the snake strikes. Think that's a coincidence?"

"Coincidence or not. I want Booker's head on a platter — now! Not three years of legal bullshit from now. I don't want him in prison. I want him dead."

"Then let's you and me take care of things, the Duke way. Let's clear the deck. That's the reason David sent me over here. I fix things. Do you have a problem with that?"

"Not as long as we don't get caught."

"Do you think this's my first rodeo? If so, you're wrong."

CHAPTER 34

The Bookers' doorbell rang. It was Tubby Butler.

"Oh, hi, Torrence ... Uh, I mean Tubby," Ace said unenthusiastically. "What's up, doc? You know we've got to quit meeting like this. People are going to start talking."

"They already are. May I come in?"

"Sure. I just fixed a fresh pot of coffee. Want some?"

"That sounds good."

Ace led Tubby back to the pass-through in the kitchen and motioned for him to take a seat as he got out a coffee cup and poured some coffee into it.

"Did you know somebody shot Faith Alice Duke?"

"Not surprising. The bitch dead?"

"She's in ICU. Got her in the shoulder. I don't guess you'd know anything about that?"

"Why is it every time something happens to one of those Pogues, I'm the first person you think of?"

"You, of all people, ought to know the answer to that."

"The last time I saw the bitch was when she was over here trying to beat up my wife after that nasty juvenile delinquent of hers pulled that bullshit on Matty at school."

"Do you own a gun?"

"Matter of fact, I do.... And, before you ask, it's legal.... Got a CCW permit.... Never know when you might need one with those rednecks around."

"Nine millimeter?"

He purposely didn't mention the nine millimeter in the top of the closet. He didn't even know when he'd last had it out, and he wasn't about to let Tubby leave him with no gun at all in the house.

"Matter of fact it is. Oh, come on now, Tub ... you can't possibly think I'd try to kill that bitch ... as much as I'd be doing the world a favor."

"Mind if I take it in and do a ballistics test on it?"

"Yes, I do mind, but I have nothing to hide."

"It's either that, or I'll have to get a search warrant."

Ace went to retrieve the pistol in the bar.

Tubby thanked him and left to take it to be analyzed.

****

As Trigger left the scene of the crime, he thought about what to do with the pistol. He decided that his first inclination to dispose of it may have been hastily made. What he really needed to do was to put the pistol back where he had found it in Ace's bedroom closet as soon as possible and let the sheriff's department find it there.

Yep. Need to get it back ASAP since, that'll probably be one of the first places the sheriff will go to look for a weapon ... if he's worth his salt.

Trigger briefly wondered whether he'd killed the witch or not but quickly dismissed trying to find out. The way he was looking at it, killing her would be doing her husband a favor. Truth of the matter was, other than the inconvenience it was causing him, it really didn't make a whole hell of a lot of difference.

If I'd been married to that bitch, I'd have killed her a long time ago. Oh, well. It's bound to be on the news.

Trigger thought Ace probably had the gun registered, if so they were sure to find it like he did when they searched Ace's house. An anonymous phone call from him should insure that. And a ballistics test would tie the gun back to the crime. Then Ace would be arrested, and he could collect the money the Triad owed him. He'd decide what he wanted to do about that asshole Earl Duke later.

Sounds like a workable plan to me. One more thing for me to do. Christ! Is this job ever gonna wind up?

CHAPTER 35

Ace brooded as he walked from the dock to the house. When he walked into the den, Matty was listening to some streamed music on his iPhone with his ear buds on.

"Matty ..."

Matty either didn't hear him or chose to ignore him.

"Son, I need to talk to you."

Matty continued to ignore him so he walked over and nudged his shoulder before walking around into Matty's line of vision.

"Now."

"What you need, dad? Can it wait until I get back? Mom and I are getting ready to leave."

"Have you been in the top of my closet?"

"Why would I do that?"

"You tell me. I don't go through your stuff."

Jo Ann heard the exchange from the bedroom and walked in to see what Ace was talking about.

Ace turned to her and said, "Did you get my pistol out of the top of our bedroom closet?"

"Why would I do that? I wouldn't know what to do with it anyway."

"Because it's missing, that's why."

"Ace, what's going on?" Jo Ann asked.

Ace noticed she was dressed like she was getting ready to go somewhere.

"What's going on is that Faith Alice Duke's been shot, and she's in the hospital. Tubby Butler came by earlier before you two got home and, as much as anything, accused me of being involved. I let him take the pistol in the bar in for ballistics tests, but I didn't mention the one on the closet shelf. It's none of his damned business. I checked after he left, and it's not in its pistol case in our closet where it's supposed to be. Either one of you know anything about that?"

"Don't look at me. You know that I don't even like guns of any sort."

"Well, somebody does, because it's gone. We must have had a break-in and been robbed."

"Have you told anyone else you had a pistol up there?" Jo Ann asked.

"Not a soul."

"Funny you should mention something odd being missing. You know that old knife that used to belong to my grandmother? I was looking for it in the drawer where I keep my odds and ends of kitchen utensils. I can't find it. I thought maybe you'd taken it to use for something and haven't brought it back. I've been meaning to ask both of you about it."

"I haven't touched it. About the only knives I use are my fillet knives and my Old Timer pocket knife, and I don't keep them in that drawer. That's your stuff. Matty, have you seen your mama's knife?"

"Don't look at me. I'm not even sure which knife you're talking about."

"This is getting stranger by the minute. Either of you missing anything else?"

"Not that I know of."

"Check your jewelry to be sure. I'm going to check the doors and windows to see if I can see any sign of a break-in.... You're dressed up like you're getting ready to go somewhere."

"Mr. Dailey, Matty's principal, called. They're getting ready to readmit that delinquent David Duke, and he wants to talk to all of us before it happens. I was hoping you'd come along."

"Mind if I beg off? I still need to wash down the boat, and then I'd need to take a shower. I'm hot and sweaty, sunburned, and I smell like fish. Besides that I'm bushed. The wind was a bitch today. All I want to do right now is to drink a beer, catch my breath, and take a quick nap before I tackle the boat. Do you mind if I pass this time? You two go. After all, you're the one who've been dealing with Dailey. You can bring me up to date when you get back."

"I do mind, but I'll explain why you're not there to Mr. Dailey. I'll get you a beer out of the fridge."

"Appreciate it. Turn the lights out when you go.... Love you."

Jo Ann got Ace's beer out of the fridge and he sat down in his recliner. Before he could drink it, he had dozed off.

****

Trigger came by shortly after Jo Ann and Matty left. He noted that Ace's truck was there, but all the lights seemed out in the house. He had no way of knowing that Tubby had already been there.

I need to get this pistol back where I got it ASAP before that deputy gets over here. Once that pistol is found missing, it won't be worth a damn to frame Booker. You know that this is gotta be one of the first places the deputy investigates. It would be if I was him. What you wanna bet that back slider I used to get in before is still unlocked. I'll be in and back out in nothing flat.

When he slipped silently into the dark house, he didn't notice Ace asleep in the recliner and quickly scooted through to Ace and Jo Ann's bedroom with the pistol in his pocket. As he reached into the top of the closet for the pistol box, a fist rocked the side of his head. He instinctively turned and threw up his forearms like an offensive tackle getting ready to block a defensive tackle. He tried to use his fist on his attacker as a hammer, but Ace slipped to the side and pushed the hammerlike fist down and away. Ace caught Trigger's head with both hands and slammed it backwards into the closet shelf. The shelf buckled and its contents spilled.

Within a half a second, even though things seemed to be going in slow motion, Trigger recovered enough to try to spring forward. Ace caught him with a second shot to his face and grabbed his hair, jerking him to the floor. The stolen pistol clattered out of his pocket. Both men reached for it. Ace got there first. The room went black as Trigger slumped down to the floor as Ace crashed the pistol down on his skull.

When Trigger's throbbing head began to clear, he tried to move his arms to no avail. He found himself duct-taped to the bedroom rocking chair. Ace stood in front of him brandishing the pistol.

"OK, Mr. John Perkins ... or whatever your name really is ... we need to have a discussion. And if I don't like what I hear, I'm going get the deputy put back over here to press charges ... after I finish beating the shit out of you and saying it was done while I was trying to detain you for breaking into my house. Maybe I'll even fabricate a story about attempted murder. It'd be my word against yours, and you're both armed and not local and broke into my house. I'd be within my rights. Even if you beat the raps, ... and I doubt you would ... it would be a long, hard, expensive battle. Am I being clear?"

"Fuck you."

Ace grabbed Trigger's hair and slapped and backhanded him one way and then the other.

"Eat me."

Ace rocked him again. Trigger's nose began to bleed. The next shot was to Trigger's groin.

He groaned and would have doubled over if he had not been so securely taped to the chair. He grimaced in pain and felt sick like he wanted to vomit. Ace pushed the rocker back and forth with his foot, making Trigger's head swim.

This hurts worse than a gunshot.

A puddle began to form on the floor under the rocking chair.

"One more time. Are you ready to begin explaining."

"You're going to regret this."

"Pardon me. I'll be right back."

Ace went into the kitchen and came back with Jo Ann's meat tenderizing hammer and her plastic cutting board.

"See these. I'm about to tenderize your fingers one at a time until tell me what's going on. Which finger do you want me to start with?"

"OK, OK! I was paid to make sure you don't testify in the Alpha Partners case against Truong Van Cam."

"Oh yeah! How much am I worth?"

"A hundred grand dead and sixty grand if neutralized as a threat," Trigger said, padding the second number by ten grand.

"Do you care where your money comes from?"

"Not anymore. I just want to get paid and get the hell out of this shithole. I don't care if I get paid by the devil himself."

"What if I told you that I have access to money that nobody knows about that'll make sure you get your payday, and that I'll not only match what they were going to pay but pad it by ten grand? All you've got to do to earn it is leave me and my family alone."

"You got my attention. We talking a hundred and ten or seventy?"

"Seventy. Don't go getting greedy on me."

"But they've got to be convinced you're no longer a threat. Otherwise I'm up shit creek, and you will be too since they'll just send someone else."

"And if they're convinced, you get to double dip."

"I wasn't going to bring that up. But why should you care? The extra money ain't coming out of your pocket."

"Of course I don't I don't give a rats ass. Double dip all you want. I don't give a shit. That's between you and them. Now, are we partners or not?"

"Yeah, partners ... once I see a downpayment. Now, let me go. We've just got to plan this out so we don't get caught. If we did, it would not work out well for either of us."

"By the way, I don't want my wife to know about this. I don't want her to see us together and for her to start pestering me to find out why."

"You got it."

CHAPTER 36

The thought of getting paid twice for the same job and only having to do it once ... with no one being the wiser ... made Trigger almost salivate. A fitting way to wind up an illustrious career.

Some people get a gold watch when they retire. I'll settle for a tax-free cash bonus. Being self-employed, After all, I don't have an IRA rollover, he grinned and thought.

And when all's said and done, he reasoned that would help make up for all the unexpected crap he'd been going through here recently.

Maybe this job won't turn out to be so bad after all. But my satisfaction won't be complete until I've settled with Earl Duke for trashing my truck. Shooting Faith Alice since she was kin to him was fine and dandy, but Duke was really the man I've been wanting to settle a score with.

Trigger didn't know it but wounding Faith Alice had already partially settled the score since she'd been responsible for Duke being in Crawfordville to begin with and had been his co-conspirator once he got there. He would've been doubly pleased if he'd known that.

Trigger began to stalk Duke. He didn't want to kill Duke prematurely and screw up his deal with Ace by having to flee town prematurely, but he wanted to be ready to write the final chapter on this job as his last official act before blowing this pissant backwater town.

"I don't want to ever come back to this shit-shack," he pronounced aloud to himself.

But Duke had to pay. In Trigger's world, scores were always settled. That was the price of disrespect. He didn't want this loose end to nag at him with why-didn't-you memories. And knowing himself very well, he knew it would otherwise.

In the meantime, Earl Duke had begun casing Ace's house so he wouldn't miss his opportunity for his own revenge.

"If that bullet had hit a vital area other than Faith Alice's shoulder, she'd be dead now and I'd have to live with the regret. I owe Haskell that much. After all, Haskell's a Duke, and Dukes take care of their own."

Even though Haskell was more than willing to participate in Ace's demise, Earl knew that since Haskell owned a business in this town and had to live there with his family, he'd be doing Haskell a favor if he just took care of this matter without involving him. Then he could return to Louisiana with a clear conscience and have David's respect. David's respect meant a lot.

Trigger noted that Earl kept on going by Ace's house several times a day. He couldn't let anything happen to Ace, or he wouldn't be able to collect the money Ace had agreed to pay him.

Earl's surveillance began to pay off before the week was out. He began to get the Booker family's routine down pat. He knew when Jo Ann went to her part time job at the bank, and when she normally returned. He knew the hours Matty was in school. He'd gotten pretty good at telling when Ace was home alone. His plan wasn't a fancy one where a lot of things could go wrong. He'd just kill him and make it look like a robbery. But he needed to do it sooner rather than later if he hoped to keep Haskell out of the picture. After all, he was a professional, and then Haskell could go back to doing what he did best — running his business.

"The main thing is Faith Alice will, by God, be avenged."

As Earl stalked Ace, he had no idea that Trigger was stalking him as well, looking for his opportunity to even his own score. The stalker was being stalked.

As Earl and Trigger watched, Ace walked from the dock back into the house to answer the call of nature. He left a radio on. John Prine was singing "Fish and Whistle." Earl used this as a sign that Ace wouldn't be gone long and slipped into the boathouse with his pistol in his hand. He'd ambush Ace when he returned and then quickly turn the contents of Ace's house upside down, making it look like an armed robbery. As he waited, Trigger slipped across the yard unnoticed and hid behind an azalea bush next to the boathouse. Normally Trigger wouldn't have had a problem with Earl taking out Ace, but he couldn't take a chance that Ace might be killed before he could collect his money. He could take a picture of Ace's body with his iPhone and claim that he'd been the assassin, thereby probably collecting from the Triad, but he wouldn't get that second paycheck he was counting on. And on top of that, this wasn't where he had hoped to ambush Earl. Too many variables. He then would have the problem of disposing of Earl, or Earl's body might maybe muddy the waters. Plus if he let Earl get away, he still wouldn't have settled that score, and he'd have to find another opportunity to square things with him. What a dilemma?

Why can't things ever be simple?

Plan "A" was for Earl to shoot Ace, but after he saw Ace's fillet knife, he decided to use it instead. Pistols make an awful racket; knives are silent giving him more time to ransack the house as he originally planned and then to get cleanly away. As Trigger watched, Earl picked up the knife, testing it for balance. Ace's body wouldn't be found until hours later, and by then Earl wouldn't even be close to this place and would have an alibi. He reasoned that it shouldn't be a problem for an experienced knife man like him since he had the advantage of surprise on his side and the radio would serve as a distraction. Plus he was up against an amateur — a desk jockey turned fisherman. He clearly had a distinct advantage, putting the odds safely on his side. He'd wait until Ace had his back turned. He'd then rush out and get him from behind. It'd be all over before Ace ever knew what hit him.

Trigger was armed, but he too didn't want to risk the attention to the situation the noise might potentially bring. He sure as hell didn't want to get caught with either body if he didn't have to. When he saw that Earl planned to use a knife, he quietly slid his belt out of his pant loops. He wrapped it around his hand, leaving the buckle swinging loose.

When Earl emerged from the boathouse with the fillet knife in his hand preparing to attack, Trigger came out from behind the bush and swung the belt trying to knock the knife out of Earl's hand. His swing caught on a limb, and came in high, however. He caught Earl in the Adam's apple instead. Earl dropped the knife and reached up for his neck, jerking the belt out of Trigger's hand.

To save the situation before it could get out of hand, Trigger sprang and tackled Earl like a linebacker drilling a quarterback from the blind side. It was a clean shoulder-to-shoulder hit that arched Earl's spine. Earl tried to retrieve the knife but kicked it instead, sending it skittering across the yard. Trigger kept coming, driving his legs, finishing the hit.

When both men hit the ground, Trigger smashed an elbow into the side of Earl's skull and hit the soft spot high on the temple. He then slapped his right palm down on Earls face, shattering his nose. His next shot clawed Earl's face in the opposite direction, driving the broken nose into Earl's brain. Earl shuddered and spasmed. Earl's face ended up with a three-finger gash that made it look like it had been mutilated by handheld garden trowel rake. Blood was beginning to pool in the cuts. In the second downward movement that followed, Trigger's index fingernail accidentally caught in one of Earl's eye sockets, gouging out that eye. The dislodged eye now hung on one end by what was left of the optic nerve. The other end was stuck to the tip of Trigger's finger, hanging grotesquely with his fingernail still penetrating Earl's eyeball. It looked like a runny egg. Trigger had to shake his hand several times to jar it loose. It finally popped loose and now sat oozing blood and staring from top of what remained of Earl's bloody eye socket. His mouth gaped through the partially torn lips that Trigger's fingernails had also raked. He could still catch a semi recognizable glimpse of what was left of Earl's face through the carnage.

Earl's battle had been over and lost and he had died before he even realized what was happening to him.

It had all happened so fast that Ace was still trying to comprehend what he had just seen.

Ace gasped and tried to speak, but only partial words came out. His breath caught in his throat as he tried not to retch at the sight. He wanted to look away but found himself staring instead.

Earl's bowels had let loose, filling the air with a revolting smell that once again almost made Ace puke. Earl had also vomited on himself before he died, and it ran down his chin.

Trigger was so out of breath that he had trouble speaking to try to answer what he thought Ace was asking.

"He was going to ..." was all he could get out in between puffs.

Ace tried to help him up, but Trigger's knees buckled and he went down again.

"Give me a mo ...," he gasped in an unfinished sentence.

"Just lie there and catch your breath."

When Trigger's heartbeat returned to normal, he said, "If you'll help me, I think I can get up now."

As Trigger got back on his feet and then slumped down in one of Ace's lawn chairs, Ace noticed a wet spot on his pants where his bladder had let loose.

"Would a beer help?"

Trigger nodded. Ace sprinted for the house. By the time he returned, Trigger was able to speak."

"Did you call the sheriff while you were in there?"

"No."

"Good. It'd be better for everyone involved if we just got rid of the body. I don't want people asking questions."

Without admitting that he had been down this road before more than once, Ace said, "Why don't we use my boat and take him out to sea?"

"Fine with me."

"Let's get busy before Jo Ann and Matty get home this afternoon. What about his truck?"

"Leave that problem for the sheriff to try to figure out. You don't want to risk driving it and being seen or having your fingerprints found in it. Right now you've got deniability on your side. C'mon. Let's get busy."

CHAPTER 37

"The safest thing to do," Trigger said, "is to mutilate the body so it can never be recognized."

"How do you propose we do that?"

"I see you've got a chum grinder."

"It's not heavy duty enough to grind bones and all, but I have a wood mulcher that is heavy enough."

"Got some heavy duty trash bags to cut on?"

"Got some visqueen."

"Even better. Go get it and spread it out on the ground."

"Got a chain saw."

"No. Too loud."

"Got a circular saw and an extension cord. Blade's not too sharp. We can plug it into the fish table."

"Who gives a rat's ass about the blade as long as it'll cut? We're not building cabinetry. Neatness don't count. Long as it works, it should be perfect. And since it's a piece of shit anyway, we'll dump it when we're done."

"I don't think I'm up to sawing him up. I think I might puke."

"I'm not surprised. I'll take care of that. Got an old ice chest you don't mind throwing away?"

"All of mine are pretty ratty."

"Do they have your name anywhere on them?"

"Nope."

"Good. Then get one to catch the ground up body pieces when they come out of the wood mulcher. Your stomach up to that, college boy?"

Ace nodded.

"Then why do you look green?"

Trigger laughed at Ace's discomfort.

"Oh, and don't plan on bringing the ice chest home. I'm going to sink it too along with the visqueen and our splattered clothing. You got a cordless Sawzall? Oh, and grab a utility knife too."

"Yes."

"Then don't just stand there. Go get them. Got any bleach to clean up the wood mulcher and boat later?"

"There's some Clorox in the house."

"Then let's get on it. The sooner this asshole becomes fish food the better. Also, ... I almost forgot, get something that we can scoop the body chum out of the ice chest with."

"Will an empty coffee can do?"

"Works for me. Better than getting my hands gooey. Let's get busy."

Ace shuddered at the thought of grabbing slimy human innards and chipped up bone with his bare hands.

By this time the odor had begun to attract all sorts of insects — flies, gnats, and mosquitos. They all flocked to the remnants of Earl's body, beginning to feed on his dead tissue and lay eggs in the warm gore. It was as if they were beginning to devour him from the inside out.

Less than an hour later the grisly remains of Earl Duke's dismantled body filled the ice chest. The body and limbs had been rent apart by the circular saw. Trigger took the skull he had just cut in half with the saw and then pounded the segments with Ace's hatchet, knocking out most of Earl's teeth in the process. The remnants of Earl's head oozed gray brain matter, and Earl's other eye had popped out of its socket. It seemed to stare at Trigger until he whacked it with the hatchet. It was now flattened into an unrecognizable gory goo. Most things had been run through the wood chipper. A gross mess of guts had spilled out onto the visqueen. Fortunately, the visqueen had been big enough to contain the largest portion of Earl's crimson blood. The ice chest contents were already beginning to look like spoiled ground beef and the accompanying tomato sauce waiting to be spread by a satanic chef in between grotesque lasagna sheets being prepared for baking. Some of the bone fragments floating on the vile surface even remotely looked somewhat like clumps of ricotta cheese.

As Ace stared at the ice chest's contents, he briefly thought about Sweeny Todd. One thing was certain. Earl Duke would trouble no one ever again because Earl Duke was no more.

When done, Trigger and Ace each grabbed a handle on the ice chest and loaded it into the stern of Ace's boat. Ace waded up the visqueen and stuffed it into an oversized contractors' garbage bag. He then retrieved a couple of his old t-shirts and old bathing suits from the house. Next he gave their work area an initial washdown. This included the blood-splattered Trigger. When Ace was done, Trigger then hosed him down as well, and they stuffed both of their grim clothing into the garbage bag they had used for the visqueen. He'd scrub up better later.

Ace was glad he'd be driving the boat and wouldn't be the one scooping the smelly offal into the water. His breath caught again in his throat, and he tried not to retch when he got near the ice chest. The stench of blood, vomit, and feces invaded his senses. The smell and sight were almost overpowering. They would not be easily forgotten. This was much worse than the other bodies Trigger didn't know about that Ace had simply weighed down and hauled intact out to sea. Even though he had washed the lawn down, in his imagination Ace still thought he saw a diluted red liquid river. He prayed for this whole experience to be over as soon as possible and wondered if God would ever forgive him.

Ace was snapped back to reality by Trigger, who shoved him from behind, saying, "Don't freeze up on me now, college boy. Get that boat cranked, and let's get the hell out of here while the getting's good."

They untied the boat and headed out to into the Gulf with their macabre cargo. Ace didn't slow down until they were about a mile out. He looked around. There were no other boats on the horizon so he dropped the boat into idle. Trigger waited until they stabilized and quit rocking until he could regain his balance before reaching into the ice chest and getting the first coffee can full of Earl's gory remains. The wind had kept the smell down while they were moving, but now it returned, almost overpowering both of their senses. Flies seemed to appear out of nowhere. Ace once again felt vile rising in his throat at the dreadful sight but repressed it by looking in the opposite direction.

Shortly after the second scoop of Earl's still moist remains hit the water, thousands of fish seemed to come out of nowhere. As a second generation fisherman, Ace had seen feeding frenzies before as predatory fish went after bait fish or chum, but this may have been Trigger's first experience with both. He reacted by involuntarily jerking backwards, dropping the coffee cup back into the ice chest. To him, it seemed that there were literally thousands of fish of almost every variety literally climbing over each other to get to the food he had just dumped into the water. Every so often a larger tail might slap the water's surface as the fish fought for the same prey. A pool of Earl's now watered-down blood spread on the Gulf's surface. Trigger had been about to ladle a third coffee can of Earl's revolting remains into the water but now said instead, in what was for him a rare admission, "Let's get the hell out of here before I lose my lunch."

"Sit down and hold on."

Before Ace could get back to the steering wheel, Trigger threw one more awful coffee can load out, this time trying to get smelly amalgamation of ground body parts and organs farther away from the boat than he had the first two times. Almost instantaneously more marine life thrashed around with their snouts elevating and their backs arched. This time they were joined by a few sharks. It was if they had all lost their minds, biting anything that got in their way in an uncontrollable rage.

Ace didn't slow again until they were about half a mile away. Once again, it appeared that they had the Gulf to themselves. Trigger ladled out several more scoops of the sickening devil's cannibalistic human stew. This time he wanted to finish the job and empty the ice chest. Their welcoming committee this time consisted mostly of sharks. Trigger threw out the jagged fragments of Earl's skull and the larger bones that that the wood chipper had left more or less intact. Tendons still connected one knee joint. These were the pieces that Trigger hadn't wanted to take the time to run through the mulcher again since they would just create more gore for Ace to clean up after later.

With explosive kicks from their mighty tails sometimes rocking the boat, the sharks surged toward the carnage only to join other sharks who had beaten them to it. They gorged themselves on whatever they could chomp on, including each other. Whereas they might normally be solitary diners, it seemed like they were saying, "Hey, that smells like a great snack" as they rammed their way through the crowd, gnashing their jaws as they tried to make sure they at least got a nibble.

And then as fast as it had begun, it was over, the sharks having gobbled up their appalling dinner, only leaving a few unsatisfying bits. Unsatiated, they circled away but didn't leave the area, hoping Trigger would provide them with another gourmet dining feast.

When Ace saw that the ice chest was empty, he told Trigger to once again hang on. He wanted to get as far away from this hideous scene as soon as possible. While Trigger didn't want to show weakness by saying it out loud, he felt the same way.

Now they had one last job to do, find a third location to cut up the ice chest and sink it. He headed for Apalachicola Bay. It took Ace less than an hour to make the nautical six-mile crossing of Apalachicola Bay. Above the reeds, silver tin roofs flashed between runs of rolling pine. He passed by Highway 98. They motored past the sleepy, water-aged riverfront. Shrimp boats of every color of flaking paint lined the bank, tied up to listing, sun-desiccated docks. Ace thought about how wonderful it would be if this could had been a pleasure cruise with Jo Ann instead of a nauseous cruise with Trigger, and the two of them could stop and eat a dozen oysters and drink a few beers. But not today. He still had other fish to fry.

A dredging pipeline ran along the channel from the Cut to Apalachicola, attended by barges and tugs. The grease and rust, thick ropes, and cast-iron cleats contrasted with Ace's stark white fiberglass boat. As he passed one barge, they saw two workers in tattered jeans, gray t-shirts, and survivor orange jackets sitting on spools of cable. They were hunched over, gazing into their phones, oblivious to the fact that Ace and Trigger were passing within fifty feet of them.

Their indifference towards the Aquaholic underscored Ace's decision to make this area the last stop for the ice chest and the bag of bloody visqueen and blood-spattered clothing. At an isolated place in the bay, Ace stopped again and Trigger used the Sawzall to carve the ice chest into pieces that would sink. Even if they didn't, they would be useless to law enforcement. He then got their awful, blood and guts spattered clothing out and slashed the items with the utility knife. The clothing reeked with the smell of death. Ace moved the boat down a little bit further and Trigger slashed the visqueen and plastic bag into ribbons. Now it was time to head home and do a final cleanup before Jo Ann and Matty returned.

CHAPTER 38

The Bookers' doorbell rang, and Jo Ann answered it. It was Tubby Butler. "Mind if I come in?"

Before she could reply, Tubby invited himself in.

"Ace here?"

"He's watching TV in the den."

"Who is it, honey?" Ace called out from the den.

"Deputy Butler."

Ace came in barefooted and dressed in an old t-shirt and gym shorts and said, "Don't you have a home, Tubby? I swear, I think you spend more time at my house than you do at your own. What now? Whatever it is, I didn't do it. But long as you're here, pull up a chair."

"Thanks. Got a couple of things for us to talk about. First of all, Faith Alice just got released from the hospital. Someone shot and wounded her."

"Too bad they only wounded her. The world wouldn't miss one less Pogue. So what does this got to do with me?"

"You ask that after the shit-storm you've had going with the whole family since you hit town? Her husband said that someone saw a white pickup drive away after she was shot."

"Oh, gimme a break! You know how many white pickups there are in this county? I haven't laid eyes on that low-life bitch since the day she and Jo Ann got into it here at the house. And if I have my way, I'll never lay eyes on her again. Jo Ann recently had another meeting with Mr. Dailey over at the high school about that teenage thug and future useless adult, David, that she's raising, but I didn't go to it."

Tubby turned to Jo Ann and asked, "Mind telling me what that meeting was all about?"

"Not at all. You know he got suspended, don't you, for picking on our son. Mr. Dailey was getting ready to readmit David to school, but he wanted to talk to us before he did so. It was just me and him. Faith Alice had met with him separately at different time."

"So y'all didn't have words?"

"She wasn't even there, and if she had been, I wouldn't have anyway unless she started something. David did get readmitted."

"So neither one of you have had any contact with her?"

"Nope and don't want to."

"Still have a gun in the house?"

"Keep one in the bar. You know that. Got to with white-trash like her and her kinfolk running around."

"Mind showing it to me again?"

Ace retrieved it and said, "Take it with you if you want. I've got nothing to hide."

Tubby looked at it and said, "That won't be necessary. It's the wrong caliber to be the gun I'm looking for."

"You said there were two things. What else can I do you for?"

"Faith Alice reported that Earl Duke, who's been visiting with them, has seemingly disappeared. We found his truck abandoned, but no Earl."

"No signs of violence? Surprising. Those Dukes run with a pretty rough crowd. If you expect me to miss him or speak at his funeral, you've come to the wrong place."

"His truck was found out here on Alligator Point not too far from here."

"So what?"

"I have to ask myself why every time something concerning that family occurs you seem to be on the periphery."

"Damned if I know why. Maybe we're both snakebit. If that's all, can I go back and finish my TV show?"

"Ace, I'll be in touch, but let me warn you, if you're involved in some kind of revenge project against the Pogues, sooner or later you're going to screw up, and I'll be there when you do."

"I'll keep that in mind. And thanks for the advice, Tubby."

After the deputy left, Jo Ann asked Ace, "Were you telling him the truth? You don't know anything about what he was asking about?"

"Not a thing, my dear, I was as surprised as you were."

"Well, just to be on the safe side, we better take extra precautions. These Pogues are crazy as a sprayed cockroach . No telling what they'll do."

"I plan to."

CHAPTER 39

"The doctor plans to release you from the hospital today," Haskell said as he sat by Faith Alice's bed. "He says that it's just going to take time for your shoulder to heal, and your arm's going to be in that sling for a while yet. But when it's all over, you're going to be fine."

"It aches constantly, and this damned sling is already getting old."

"That's why he's giving you a prescription for a pain medication."

"I'd love to kill the son of a bitch who did this to me."

"Let's not talk about that here. You never know when there might be prying ears. We'll discuss it on the way home. Let me just say this. We're pretty sure Earl was the target, and you were just at the wrong place at the wrong time. But enough for now. We'll talk about it in the truck."

After what seemed like forever, the paperwork was finally in place so Faith Alice could be discharged. An orderly took her out to their truck in a wheelchair. They then left to return to Crawfordville.

"So, who'd be after Earl?" Faith Alice asked.

"Could be a lot of people. You know, Earl Duke's not exactly popular in a lot of circles. And now he seems to have disappeared."

"You think he chicken-shitted out and went back to Louisiana? ... Damn it, Haskell. Drive carefully. Those bumps you're hitting hurt. "

"Sorry. I didn't pave this road.... No. That wouldn't be like him. That boy's seen more shit in his life than a goose with diarrhea."

"Have you tried to call him?"

"Of course. I may be stupid, but I'm not dumb. Doesn't answer. He told me something at the hospital though before he hauled ass or whatever. He couldn't see the shooter, but the shooter was driving a white RAM. You know who owns one of those, don't you?"

"That turd, Ace Booker. And you haven't done anything about it?"

"Tubby Butler talked to him, but of course he denied everything. And my main concern was making sure the doctors did everything possible to patch you up."

"If you're any kind of man, you won't let this go unanswered. You won't let him get away with this."

"Don't plan to. Like I said, my main concern up until now has been you.... And trying locate Earl."

They drove along silently for a while. Faith Alice winced every time Haskell hit a bump.

"Let's burn his house down," Faith Alice suddenly blurted out.

"Are you serious?"

"Serious as a bullet in the shoulder. You've got some lawnmower gas in the shed behind the house, don't you? And I want to be there when you do it. And I mean sooner rather than later if you want to get along with me."

Haskell wasn't comfortable with Faith Alice's plan, but he said nothing. They'd been married long enough to know you couldn't reason with her when she got like this.

The following morning Ace was almost home, returning from the Walmart Super Center. Jo Ann and Matty had left for the morning. Then, as he approached his house, he saw Haskell's truck parked out front with motor running. Faith Alice was in it. His hackles immediately went up. Then he saw Haskell walking across his yard carrying a plastic gas can.

Those crazy people mean to burn us out.

He floored his truck and took off across his front yard. It took a few moments to get traction, leaving a rut and a cloud of unrooted, newly cut grass behind him before the truck caught hold and surged forward again.

I'll mow Haskell down if I have to.

Haskell saw Ace's truck barreling towards him and dropped the gas can. He took off running, screaming at the top of his lungs.

"Faith! Faith!"

Even though she only had one usable arm, she slid across the seat to the driver's side.

Ace hit the plastic gas can, spraying gas everywhere. The smashed gas can bumped up under his truck, the racket causing him to momentarily hesitate.

Haskell beat him to the truck and leaped into the passenger side just before Ace could get to him.

"Go! Go! Let's get the hell out of here."

Faith Alice floored the truck, driving with her good arm, and it leaped ahead on Sunset Hideaway with Ace only moments behind. Only then did she notice that they had left the truck pointing in the wrong direction. Instead of heading back to the mainland, they were on Alligator Drive headed towards the dead end at the foot of the peninsula. It was too late to try to turn around now, but somehow, she had to try to do it. For the first time that morning, she was scared.

Ace, fueled by fury, continued to accelerate and began to close the gap between the two trucks. Fortunately for both, they were the only vehicles on the isolated road.

Suddenly, a deer darted into the road.

Faith Alice swerved, and the speeding truck went airborne as she tried to avoid it. Faith Alice felt the collar bone on her already wounded shoulder shatter when it hit. She passed out at the wheel.

Haskell was thrown through the windshield. He skittered across the pavement face down.

Ace braked just in time to not be part of the collision. He looked around. There were no witnesses. He speed-dialed Trigger and told him where they were.

"I'm not far away. Be there in two minutes or less. Anyone see the accident?"

"No."

"Are they dead?"

"Don't know."

"Got your pistol with you?"

"Of course."

"Then make sure they're dead. Put a bullet in each of their heads to make sure. I'm almost to you."

"I ... ."

"Don't wimp out now, college boy."

Before he could get his pistol out of the glove compartment, Trigger's truck came racing down the road, and he jumped out.

"Did you do what I told you to do?"

"Not yet!"

"Then give me that damned pistol."

Trigger walked over to truck and jerked the driver's side door open. Faith Alice was slumped over the wheel, but her convulsing body told him that she was still alive. He fired twice tearing a hole in both of her gut and her head. The bullets lodged in the passenger side door after they passed through her body. A sudden rush of mangled, paled and glistening intestines and blood with the combined consistency of cottage cheese erupted. Some of the intestines looked like unwrapped raw sausages. Her brain matter clung to the interior of the truck like fragments of greyish scrambled eggs. The gory goo spattered out as well on both his face and shirt. He nonchalantly wiped his face with his shirt sleeve and tucked the pistol in his belt. With one hand grasping the steering wheel for support, he dragged her now dead body out of the truck with his other hand and dumped it unceremoniously onto the asphalt and away from the truck. Her thick blood and mangled guts left a grisly trail behind her.

Trigger then walked over to where Haskell lay face down. Haskell's twitching leg told him Haskell was still alive. He kicked Haskell once to see what reaction he would get. Haskell groaned. He then stomped on the back of Haskell's left knee. He could hear both bone and cartilage shattering. Haskell groaned again. Trigger then prodded the body, partially turning it over with his foot. The features on Haskell's face had been completely obliterated by his slide across the pavement. His face looked like raw meat. He heaved as blood came out of what used to be his mouth and pooled on the remainder of his face and as well as the pavement. His shirt had been torn loose as well, exposing his bloody chest and stomach. Trigger kicked him again to test for any remaining life. Haskell's chest rose up and down. He then dragged Haskell by the heels over to where Faith Alice's body lay. A grotesque trail of blood covered the blacktop where the body had been dragged. He then took the pistol out of his belt and put one bullet through Haskell's stomach and another through the remains of his face. Haskell's bowels and bladder let loose, filling the air with a nauseous odor. The bullets lodged in the pavement beneath him.

Ace had to suppress the desire to throw up.

"I guess you know we can't leave the bodies here for the deputy and the Pogues to find, don't you? You'll be the first person everyone will suspect. You want to go to prison? If not, help me throw the bodies into the back of your truck, and let's get the hell out of here before anyone knows we were even here. Are you OK?"

"No."

"Too damned bad. Whether you are or not, I need your help. Stay with me, college boy unless you want to get what they got. This gun's not empty."

"OK! OK!"

"And you know this pistol has got to go away."

"I know."

"Then let's get busy before we have company."

They loaded the two bodies into the bed of Ace's truck.

"Now, let's get the hell out of here. We can deal with the bodies like we have before."

"I don't want to chop them up."

"Then we'll give them some concrete boots and sent them to Valhalla for a permanent vacation. Since you're a fisherman, I presume you know of some more remote locations or two."

"Of course. We'll head straight out to sea a few miles from the Bald Point State Park area."

"You can clean everything up when we get back. Right now, let's get these things disposed of."

Ace's stomach heaved again, and he began to involuntarily shake. He had never been so scared in his whole life.

"Don't wimp out on me now, college boy. You can throw up after we get back."

They did as Trigger said.

The Gulf soon had more fresh Pogue fish food.

CHAPTER 40

Several hours later, as Ace and Trigger were pulling back into the dock to conclude their macabre mission and clean up after themselves, Ace saw Tubby's car parked in his driveway.

"Just be cool," Trigger advised. "We're out of the woods now."

Tubby walked down to the dock. He had another man with him. They waited for Ace to dock.

"What do I owe the pleasure this time? Did I jaywalk or something?"

"Ha, ha. Real funny. You're not going to find it so funny when I tell you why we're here. I've got a warrant to spray Luminal on your property for blood traces."

"Wonderful. You know this is bordering on harassment, don't you? Who's the clown with you? A trainee you're teaching how to mistreat the public?"

"Let me introduce him. This is Special Agent Bowry, from the Florida Department of Law Enforcement in Tallahassee. Luminol requires special training if it's to be an effective tool, and in this county we don't have enough need of it to know enough to keep from possibly screwing up when we use it. So they lent us Agent Bowry and his partner Agent Rodrigues."

"I don't see Agent Rodrigues. Where are you hiding him?"

"Fortunately they happened to be in town in time to help Sherriff Carpenter with another crime that has just occurred today. Haskell Duke's truck was found not too far from here. From the blood stains, it was obvious that he had been murdered. There's blood stains where two bodies were dragged out of his truck. We checked, and no one has seen either him or his wife today. Right now Agent Rodrigues is at the crime scene helping Sheriff

Carpenter before it gets tainted. FDLE has a lot more experience with matters of this nature than we do.... So I guess Agent Bowry and I will have to go it alone."

"Sorry to hear that. And sorry to hear about Haskell and whoever was with him."

"Sure! I bet you are. You're hoping it's Faith Alice. Ace, you're not a very convincing liar."

"No comment. I'll just say that I guess those Pogues are snakebit, and they deserve to be. I'll leave it at that."

"They've been bit alright, but I don't think snakes are doing it ... Seems instead like a snake-in-grass to me. But one of these days that snake'll slip up and when he does ... By the way, who's your companion here. A new deckhand? I don't believe I caught his name."

"Because I didn't tell it to you."

Trigger interrupted the exchange and said, "Tom Jones."

"Like the singer?"

"No, like the cock-hound in the movie."

"A fisherman who's also a lady's man. Or is it a lady's man who knows how to fish? Multitalented. I don't think I've ever seen you around here."

"I'm from South Florida. We knew each other down there. Fish come in all shapes and sizes and varieties.... And as far as fish go, a fish is a fish even though the methods of catching them are somewhat different...."

"Speaking of fish. No fish today, Ace? I hear from your competition that catches have been pretty good lately. You losing your touch?"

Now Ace was really starting to sweat. He looked at Trigger for assistance. Trigger was mute.

"... Uh! Uh! ... Mr. Jones isn't a fisherman," Ace stammered after a pregnant pause. "I've been having some trouble with my boat engine, and Mr. Jones worked on it for me. We were taking it out for a test run to see if the problem was solved."

"Hmmm! Must have been a really bad problem if you had to bring in a mechanic from out of town. We've got some pretty good mechanics right here local."

Ace just stared trying to think of what to say next. Trigger broke in at this point.

"Like I said, I'm just visiting from South Florida, and I used to work on his boat down there. Is that a problem?"

"No. I just like to know who's who in the county. Welcome to Wakulla County. I hope you enjoy your stay. Well, now that everyone knows everyone else, Agent Bowry and I need to get busy. So if you'll excuse us ..."

This gave Trigger an excuse to get away from this conversation that was making him uncomfortable as well.

He turned to Ace and said, "I've got other things to do as well. I think we had a good test run. Now, if you'll excuse me Mr. Booker, I'll be off now. Call me if it gives you any more trouble."

He wanted to get away from there as soon as he could.

"Thanks for your help, Tom. I'll call you if I need you."

With no further comments without looking back, Trigger turned, headed for his truck, and drove away.

"Pleasant fellow," Tubby said. "Well, come on Agent Bowry. I guess we need to get busy."

"I'll be in the house."

"We'll do it first. Ace, don't plan on going anywhere."

"Whatever."

Ace tried to appear nonchalant even though he was panicking internally. After going in the house he sat in his recliner and turned on Fox News, pretending to watch it even though he wasn't listening to a word of the broadcast. His pulse throbbed in his ears, a relentless drumbeat that drowned out the TV's sound. His vision blurred. The edges of his surroundings began to warp and distort the broadcast as panic and fear clouded his perception.

Time stopped. He was jarred back into reality when Tubby said, "We're through in here now. We didn't find anything. We're going outside."

"I knew you wouldn't," Ace replied in a voice that caught in his throat. Instead of expressing confidence and his usual brashness, it was almost a strangled whisper that he was afraid was betraying the fear that had coiled up inside him. His voice was a fragile thread that threatened to snap under the weight of his self-imposed panic. He silently chastised himself for his guilty behavior after Tubby and Agent Bowry walked out the door. This only cause him to panic even more.

Even though his legs had seemed to turn to lead, he managed to get back up out of the chair. Each step seemed like a Herculean effort. It seemed that his feet and legs were dragging a ball and chain. Fear had seeped into their very bones, making each step an arduous task. He turned and looked out the sliding door into the yard towards the fish table where he and Trigger has dismantled Earl Duke's body and ground it into hellish hamburger meat. As familiar as the table and surrounding dock area were, they seemed to be turning into a nightmarish apparition.

As he watched them walk towards his truck, his heart began to hammer against his ribcage, and the thunderous beat reverberated throughout his body, matching the rhythm of his escalating panic. He clutched his chest with trembling fingers, trying to keep it from leaping out of his body.

If they spray that truck bed, that's what's going to get me caught. Damn, if only Trigger had let me wash out that truck bed before we hauled the bodies out to sea.

Ace's hands began to shake uncontrollably in an involuntary tremor that betrayed his inner turmoil as fear and panic waged a relentless battle within him. His thoughts careened through a maze of worst-case scenarios, each possibility more terrifying than the last as panic hijacked their possibility.

I'll never see my family again, but that'll be the least of my problems. I'll be publicly disgraced as a serial killer. Jo Ann will leave me. Matty will disown me. I'm going to be convicted of murder and spend the rest of my life in prison. No, I'll probably be executed or killed by another prisoner. Even if I somehow escape those nightmares, Trigger will kill me to make sure I keep my mouth shut. And if he doesn't, the Triad will send someone else up here to do it for them. My life is over. I'm dead any way you look at it.

He clamped his hands over his mouth to stifle a scream as he fought dizziness as the panic threatened to consume him.

Shadd up! I can't do that with Tubby and Agent Bowry here. It'll be a dead giveaway.

His knees began to buckle. He stumbled back to the recliner and fell into it. That was the last thing he remembered until he looked at the clock and saw several hours had elapsed.

He looked out into the yard and saw that Tubby's car was gone. He pressed his trembling hands against his temples, trying to still the frantic thoughts racing through his mind, wondering what Tubby had found. Each thought was a reminder of what was probably getting ready to come in his own snakebit existence.

CHAPTER 41

Later Ace heard a pounding on the front door. He didn't respond immediately. The pounding continued. He peeked out and saw it was Trigger.

"You deaf or something? Let me in."

Trigger shoved his way into the house.

Ace started to explain the things that had happened after Trigger had left, but Trigger cut him off.

"I don't give a shit what went down and don't want to hear you whine, college boy. One of the reasons I've survived as long as I have in this business is I know when it's time to peddle my ass down the road and fade to black. And that time is now. This whole situation is getting very uncomfortable. This deputy is getting too close for comfort. Kenny Rodgers said it well. You got know when to hold 'em and know when to fold 'em and know when the gig's up."

"It's not that simple for me."

"That's your damn problem."

"So, why are you telling me this? Why aren't you down the road?"

"Because I haven't been paid, that why. You think I live on charity and air? I've got a pretty good amount of time and money invested in this fiasco, and I'm here to collect some of what's due me."

"I can't just blink and put my hands on that kind of money."

"We had a contract. You better figure out how to do it unless you want more trouble than you ever thought existed. And you know I can back up my words with action."

"After what we've been through together, I thought we were friends."

"In my world, friends are not a luxury you enjoy. I just have occasional trustworthy associates. And if you welch, don't think your family is off limits."

"You know. That day I caught you in my house, I could have killed you."

"And I could have killed you long before that. That's what I was sent here to do, but then I got distracted. My bad. Won't happen again.

"Ace, let's get truthful for a second, you didn't kill me when you had the chance because you don't have the killer instinct. You're a pussy. You've never killed anyone in your life. Well, Ace, that's not me. I'm a professional killer who has killed plenty of times."

"You don't know me as well as you think you do."

"I'm coming back tomorrow. I expect you to be in a position to settle our account then."

"Can't make it happen that fast," Ace lied as he tried to buy time.

Only he knew that his money had been converted into gold coins. They were nontraceable, portable, liquid, and left no paper trail. Plus, a million dollars in gold coins only weighed about forty pounds.

"What *can* you do? And you better not try jerking my chain, buddy boy. What'll come next won't be pretty. What can you do?"

"Three days. That's a good as it gets."

"No sale unless you want to play with fire. Two and no more. The quicker I get out of this hellhole the better. Right now the deputy thinks I'm Tom Jones, but who knows how long that will last. And I'm not a person of interest at present. That could change real quick. If he checks my truck registration, he'll learn who I really am. And then he might start checking into my background. There's a lot of skeletons in my closet, and I want them to stay there. I plan to be long gone before any of this shit can happen. Out of sight and out of mind."

"But guess what? If you burn me during that three-day period you don't get anything. Not shit," Ace retorted. "Nada. Zip city. And there won't be a damned thing you can do about it ... because my wife don't know doodly squat about that money. By the way, asshole, I hate to remind you, but I'm still waiting on you hold up your end of the bargain. You were supposed to protect me from the Triad by faking my death. What do I do if they send someone else up here?"

"Didn't have time to do that. But now I guess that'll be your problem. Not that it's any of my business but a little free advice. I think it's time you moved on down the road too and found a new place to live. I'll be back tomorrow. No negotiation. End of story. Don't fuck with me, Ace. Better men than you have tried to and failed."

"Where can I get hold of you?"

"No, no, baby cakes. If you can find me, Deputy tub-of-lard can too in case you grow some gonads and go to him. As the adage goes, I may be dumb, but I ain't stupid. Clock's ticking."

For effect, Trigger slammed the door.

If Ace had thought he was on the verge of going mad before as he had precariously balanced over a cliff, now he felt like he had just gone over it.

CHAPTER 42

After Trigger left, Ace felt like he was carrying around the weight of the world. He honestly didn't feel any of the bravado that he had just tried to bluff Trigger with. At first he huddled against the passthrough to the kitchen, huddling against it with his arms wrapped tightly around himself, biting his lip until it almost bled. He was seeking solace in his own embrace and using his arms as a physical barrier against the encroaching fear and panic. It didn't help. His breath began to come in shallow gasps as his chest rose and fell rapidly as the weight of the fear threatened to suffocate him. He worked his way towards his recliner. Just as he reached it, his knees turned to jelly and he collapsed into it as fear continued to escalate in his veins.

His mind began to race from one worst case scenario to the next. Every possibility seemed more terrifying than the one that preceded it, causing his body to tremble uncontrollably and making his muscles quake as if he were caught in the grip of an invisible tempest.

I need a drink or I'm going to have a heart attack or stroke, he told himself.

He somehow pushed himself back out of the recliner and stumbled his way to the kitchen cupboard where he knew he'd find an open bottle of Bacardi and then inched back again.

That was the last thing he remembered until he heard Jo Ann's voice.

"Ace, you're drunk."

"Just had a nip or two," he alibied.

"No, you're shitfaced. Let me help you to the bedroom. I don't want Matty to see you looking like this."

That was the last thing he remembered for another two hours when he awoke again. He felt like shit. Jo Ann was staring over him, looking disgusted.

"Where's Matty?" Ace said.

"He's doing his homework."

"We need to talk."

"Yes, we do."

"We've got to move."

He then explained to her how Tubby Butler might show up anytime with a warrant for his arrest for some of the Pogue killings. He told her who Trigger Perkins and how he was a professional killer who been hired by the Triad to kill him to keep him from testifying against them. He told her about how he had had to come to an temporary arrangement with Trigger, but that this was not a permanent solution since the Triad could and would hire other hitmen. He told her that the Pogues feud would never abate and only escalate and rationalized how this would inevitably endanger Matty.

"They're determined to run us out of the county. And they'll do it any way they can."

"What would we live on? Your dad's house and boat are the only assets we have left, and the only reason I can bring in what income I do is because of the generosity of my dad."

"I have monies you don't know about. We'll be OK on that front."

"And what's this arrangement you've come to with the Triad killer?"

"I bought him off."

"You've got that kind of money?"

"Yes, my dear, I do."

"And I thought I was the only one living with lies. I too have a confession to make."

"You?"

"Yes, me. When we were still in Miami, I was approached by the FBI. They told me that they knew that illegal activities were going on at your firm, but they couldn't prove it yet. But they said they were determined to get the proof they needed, and that it was just a matter of time before they did so. And that when they did, everyone would be sent away for long prison terms — including you. At first I refused to cooperate."

"Thank you, my dear. I'd a done the same for you."

"But they were persistent. They told me that they planned to investigate my father as well, and that they would do it in such a public manner that even if he was exonerated his reputation and career would be over since people would always wonder."

"What could they accuse him off? He's about the straightest and most honest man I know."

"They planned to say that the two of you teamed up to purposely defraud the investors at his bank. And that you were sharing the money you were screwing them out of. Even if the charges proved to be false, they would publicize the investigation as widely as possible and then keep a lid on the details when he was exonerated. They were going to publicly hang him unless I came onboard. They also sweetened the deal by telling me that they'd make sure that you only got a slap on the wrist and that it'd be done in such a way that you would think you'd cut the deal instead of me and thereby protect your precious manhood. I finally agreed. For the sake of our family, I had to. At the time I agreed, I thought you were innocent. Now I know better."

"So what did you do?"

" I let them bug everything we own and even helped them bug your office so they could collect the evidence they needed. But one thing that they didn't tell me was that they were going to confiscate virtually everything we own since it was determined that these things were derived from what they deemed to be your illegally earned compensation."

"Did they know about the Chinese Triad?"

"They strongly suspected it. That's why they were pursuing the case as avidly as they were. But I never thought the Triad would send a hired killer up here to get even."

"All this makes even more reason that we have to go."

"No, Ace. I'm not going to do it. I am not going to raise our child on the run under assumed names. I put my foot down. I love you, but I'll divorce you first."

"But I've got enough money stashed away for us to live comfortably for the rest of our lives."

"I honestly believed you were an innocent employee. Now I know better. You're no better than the scuzzes you worked for. If I were going to do anything with that money, I'd give it to my father so he could give it back to the people it really belongs to."

"This is your final decision?"

"Yes, it is. It's not worth it to spend the rest of my life running from both the law and bunch of Asian thugs and wondering every day when one or the other is going to catch up to us and we wouldn't ever be safe no matter how much money you've stolen.... Don't tell me. I don't want to know.... But I will do this because I love you, I won't report this conversation to the police. But if they discover the truth on their own, I won't deny it either."

CHAPTER 43

Ace picked at his dinner that night in silence as he thought this might be one of his last, and quite possibly it might be his last meal with the family. Shrimp scampi was normally one of his favorites. Matty scarfed his down, seemingly oblivious to the silence of both of his parents. The tension in Ace's muscles went into a fight or flight mode and began pumping waste through his system that made his stomach feel bloated as it began to cramp. The shrimp scampi which was normally soothing and comforting to his stomach now had total different effect on him. The shrimp seemed to be using the fettuccini as a bungee cord to bounce up and down in a deliberate attempt to irritate the lining of his esophagus as his stomach butterflies egged them on.

After dinner he silently helped Jo Ann put the leftovers away and rinse the dishes. He asked Matty if he had homework to do, and when Matty said he did, Ace excused him to do it. Ace said he didn't think there was anything on TV that sounded particularly interesting so he thought if Jo Ann didn't mind he'd read some more of a novel that he was into. He retreated to the bedroom and closed the door. Ace opened the book but found that his concentration ability was almost nonexistent. When bedtime came, as much as Ace would have liked the comfort of Jo Ann's embrace, he knew it wasn't going to happen. So he said he wasn't sleepy and was just getting into the best part of the book so he'd take it into the den and read in his recliner in order to not keep Jo Ann awake. She didn't object.

All alone in the den, Ace began to panic again. His hands trembled as he tried to hold on to the book. He pressed his trembling hands to his temples, trying to still the frantic thoughts that raced through his mind, each one a taunting reminder of everything that had happened since they moved into his dad's house. His skin prickled and he broke into a clammy cold sweat. His goosebumps rose like a constellation of fear as his body sought to shield itself from the inevitable events soon to come, and he bit his lip again, almost causing it to bleed. The sharp metallic taste once again reminded him just what a calamity his life had turned into. The pain offered only a momentary distraction from the overwhelming panic threatening to consume him. He wondered if Jo Ann was feeling the same way. He couldn't relax. His eyes darted around the room. His pupils dilated as he sought answers that refused to come. The lack of answers only increased his panic and only set his nerves even more ablaze. Ace knew what he had to do. He just wasn't sure if he was up to it.

You don't have any choice. You've got to be up to being aggressive. You've to go on the offensive. Now turn out the lights before Jo Ann comes in here and wants you to explain what you can't explain if you hope to succeed.

He made a decision.

Ace stumbled to the refrigerator and got out a beer. He wasn't sure why. Was he celebrating coming to a conclusion, or was he simply trying to calm his jumbled nerves? He wasn't sure. He doused all the lights in the room and felt his way back to his recliner. He shivered in the dark, making him want to turn the thermostat down, but knew that this wouldn't stop his shivering. It would only make Jo Ann and Matty uncomfortable.

He sat in the dark sipping the beer. Instead of comforting him, it only caused his stomach to churn as "what-if's" raced through his brain. He set the beer aside before it caused him to vomit.

He suddenly felt an overwhelming desire to tell Jo Ann and Matty how much he loved them but knew that it was the wrong thing to do at this juncture. He doused the lights and felt his way across the room again to his recliner. He felt dizzy and hung on a floor lamp after a few steps to get his equilibrium back. He plopped down into it. He was panting from exhaustion of just crossing the room. Even though he had now made a decision, he felt no better. He felt an overwhelming sense of dread at what he knew he had to do. The fear felt like it was penetrating his skin and going right down to his bones. He imagined dying as an overwhelming sense of dread took charge of his brain.

I've got to get some sleep. Now, take a few deep breaths.

He tried to calm down but found himself unable to take more than shallow breaths as his heart palpitated and his dry mouth and throat threatened to close up his windpipe. An acidic taste bubbled in his throat. Finally, he jerked a sharp breath. As he sat there in the dark, be began doubting his decision, only making existing triggers intensify and new ones to develop.

What kind of future do I have to look forward to?

This only caused his panicked thoughts to grow wild and to make his blood pound in his ears. Finally, his exhausted body surrendered, and Ace fell into a coma-like, fitful sleep of sorts.

The next thing Ace remembered was looking around the room as the morning sun lit it up. He was alone in the house. Jo Ann had quietly left without waking him to take Matty to school and go to the bank. She apparently was repressing further discussion. But what was there to discuss? Her "no" had left no doubt as to her position. Was she now seeking a lawyer? At some point she'd have to speak to him again. Or was that going to be through an intermediary? Except for his mental exhaustion, this would have set off another panic attack.

OK, Ace, you've got a plan. Now put it into action.

Ace started by going down to the boathouse and retrieving the cardboard boxes of gold from their hiding place. He took some newspaper and a candle down to the boat as well. He needed to break the coins up into smaller, more portable portions. There were some airline bags and zippered overnight bags in the closet and attic. He found enough to do the job and split the gold into manageable allotments, putting some in his pocket. He made some preparations on the boat. Then he took his wheelbarrow into front yard. When that was done, he went in the house and packed a suitcase with essentials. He grabbed his passport case and the social security card that he secretly kept in his jewelry box. He then walked through the house, pausing in each room as memories were evoked. He picked up certain items that were meaningful to him and held them for a few moments. He put two stacks American Eagle $50 gold coins on Jo Ann's bedside table where she was sure to find them. All tasks having been completed, he retreated to his recliner and began to silently wait. Time slowed to a crawl as he stared out into space. At last he heard a rap on the front door.

He hesitated as thoughts raced through his mind.

There was a second impatient knuckle rap.

He still hesitated.

The rap turned into a fist pounding.

He knew who it was. When he saw the shadow through the glass he knew he was right.

When Ace opened the door, Trigger was standing there.

"You deaf or something?"

Ace did not respond but opened the door enough for Trigger to enter. He had one hand behind his back. He stepped back and to one side so Trigger could come in.

When Trigger was halfway through the door, the arm behind Ace's back darted out with his fist gripping the filet knife. He jabbed forward. Trigger was moments late in trying to block it and sweep it aside. It plunged into his gut just adjacent to his navel. Ace continued to push until the knife was up to its hilt.

Trigger looked down, shocked that he had allowed himself to be caught off guard. At first, he felt like he'd been punched in the gut, but the area around the wound began to feel ice cold and the cold feeling turned into an electric shock as if a hot iron poker was being shoved through his gut. He began to have trouble breathing. The blood was minimal at first. Ace then ripped the small hole into a gaping one by twisting the knife and opening a wound almost up to Trigger's chest. Now the blood began to pour out. Ace then pulled the knife out and jabbed again. This time through Trigger's neck. He released his hold on the knife and it protruded grotesquely from Trigger's throat. Trigger stumbled forward. Ace stiff-armed him with the heels of his hands and sent him reeling backwards into the front yard. Ace then silently watched as Trigger began to bleed out, waiting for him to die.

When Ace was sure Trigger was dead, he loaded the body into the wheelbarrow and rolled it back to the dock and unceremoniously dumped it into the boat. Ace's eulogy was his middle finger. He then loaded the bags of gold into the wheelbarrow and took them out front. This done, he went back to the house to hose down the crime scene. He left the front door open so he could wash down the tiled foyer.

It should dry by the time Jo Ann and Matty get home this afternoon.

Ace began to wheel the bags of coins out to his truck but changed his mind and took them out to Trigger's truck instead.

The final detail of his plan fell into place. He would make the world think that Trigger's incinerated body was his.

Why didn't I think of this before? No one will be able to tell the difference. Besides, Jo Ann can use this truck, and Trigger has no use for his anymore. Matty will be driving soon, and now she won't have to buy Matty a car. And the longer it takes for someone to miss Trigger — as if anyone will truly miss that dirtbag — the better it is for me. Very few people even know he's still in the county. And nobody of consequence but Tubby has ever met him anyway.

Now Ace knew he'd succeed.

When he went back down to the boat to retrieve Trigger's keys, he pocketed Trigger's wallet. He put his own wallet minus his driver's license in the boat console. This done he went back up to the house to get the suitcase of clothing and other essentials and loaded them along with the gold into Trigger's truck.

Ace had one last thing to do. He backed the boat out the boathouse and pulled it next to the dock. He'd wadded up the newspaper and scattered it on the cabin deck near the candle. With masking tape he secured the candle on top of it. He checked one last time to see if he'd forgotten anything. Everything seemed in order. Now satisfied, Ace lit the candle, cranked the engine, and headed the boat putting straight out to sea using the slowest speed he could. He then jumped back onto the dock and watched the boat slowly pull away to see if it was headed where he wanted it to go.

Everything seemed perfect.

Trigger, my almost friend, I bet you never dreamed you'd have a Viking funeral.

Out loud Ace made one last request, "Will you send me a postcard from Valhalla so that I'll know you got there, asshole?"

Ace laughed and then went back out to Trigger's truck. He opened the glovebox and saw that Trigger kept both a pistol and a knife in it.

So he wasn't armed with either when he came to the door. I guess he didn't plan to kill me today, but I'm sure the day would've come when he would've tried to do so.

Ace's conscience briefly surfaced, but he quickly repressed the regret.

What's done is done. This is the way it had to be. I had no other way out.

He turned and looked at the house and empty boat house one last time. The boat kept slowly putting out to sea.

Full tank of gas. I guess you really were planning to leave today. Thank you, Trigger. Now, let's get going.

I sure wish I had more traveling money right now instead of virtually everything being in gold. I guess you can't have everything.

CHAPTER 44

Tubby Butler shook his head as he drove down the highway. He had expected to be serving an arrest warrant for Matthew "Ace" Booker, but he was on a completely different mission instead. The blood stains the Luminol detected in the bed of Ace's truck matched the blood types of Haskell Duke and his wife Faith Alice. He had sent samples in to see if the DNA matched. He had no doubt it would. And the fingerprints extracted from the door handle on Haskell's truck had been identified. They belonged to one Robert Perkins, a former felon, last known address Miami.

He called FDLE in Miami and was told that Perkins was a pretty nasty character. Robert Perkins was his professional name. They had also heard him called Trigger Bob. His birth name was Rocco Alessandro Caputo. He had long been suspected of being a professional assassin for hire, but his one arrest had been for larceny. FDLE had been wanting to take him down for years, but so far he seemed to stay one step ahead of them. They were now thrilled to hear from Deputy Butler telling them that Caputo's fingerprints had been found at the scene of a double homicide. They had been wanting to get him off the streets for years. Maybe they finally had him. The report back on Trigger Bob convinced Tubby more than ever that Ace was somehow guilty.

So Mr. Tom Jones is Rocco Caputo, otherwise known as Trigger Bob. Boy, oh boy! I'm tell you! That Ace Booker runs with some pretty rough trade. I knew there was something about that Tom Jones guy I didn't like, and my cop instincts were right.

165

Since finding out Trigger's background, Tubby had tried to locate him, but he seemed to have just vanished.

He'll turn up. He's got to sooner or later. He can't hide forever.

But now he was travelling to the Booker residence for an entirely different reason, one even more distasteful than his original mission. And one much less satisfying. Arresting Ace Booker would have put a feather in Tubby's hat. Reporting to Jo Ann that her husband was dead had the opposite effect on him.

One decision he had made after the boat tragedy was that he would never tell anyone about what the Luminol had found and about the events that followed. He would just quietly close the file. Since Ace was dead it would serve no purpose. The only thing it would do would be to hurt the living — the remaining members of the Booker family. Maybe it would bring some closure to the Pogues, but it wasn't worth it since it would probably give them an excuse to further ruin Jo Ann and Matty's lives. Just as important, it might even jeopardize his own job since Jo Ann's father was a prominent member of the community. If as a result of this mess he decided to actively support and contribute to Sheriff Carpenter's opponent in the next election, causing the sheriff to lose, Tubby could easily be out of a job as the new sheriff brought in his own people.

Nope. It's simply not worth it. I've got little to gain and everything to possibly lose if a controversy arises. Best for everybody concerned if I stay under the radar screen and don't rock the boat.

He briefly wondered why Jo Ann hadn't reported Ace as a missing person. Did the Bookers have a strained marriage? The one thing he was absolutely certain of was that the Pogue family would celebrate Ace's demise.

I never in a million years expected the Pogue/Booker feud to end like this. It was a lot more likely that I'd be on a mission to arrest one or the other for killing or maiming someone on the other side.

When Tubby drove up in front of the Booker residence, he noted that both Jo Ann's car and Ace's truck were there. He parked, walked up the front door, and knocked on it with the doorknocker. Jo Ann came to the door.

"Jo Ann, may I come in?"

"Sure, Tub ... deputy ... But Ace isn't here. I don't know when he'll be back. I'm pretty sure he's out on his boat."

"Yes, I know he isn't here. You're the person I came to talk to."

"Is something wrong?"

"I'm afraid so. Can we talk about it in the house?"

After they sat down in the living room, Tubby said, "Jo Ann, I hate to be the one to tell you this, but Ace's boat caught fire and exploded and he was on it. The body was charred beyond recognition, but we found the remains of his wallet in the boat console with some of his ID so I'm sure it was him. I'm so sorry."

Jo Ann was speechless. Had Ace purposely blown up his boat after she refused to go on the run with him?

Finally she said, "Thank you, Tubby, for coming by and telling me. If there's nothing else you need to tell me, do you mind if I tell you I wish to be alone?"

"Not at all. I'd feel the same way. The accident will be investigated, and I'll keep you informed if we learn something you need to know. Again, I'm sorry. I've known Ace for a long time. And if there's anything I can do ... and I mean insurance companies, government agencies, anyone ... to smooth you through this period as easily as possible, all you have to do is ask. And if the Pogues give you any trouble, I want to know about it. ... I'll let myself out. I'm so sorry."

CHAPTER 45

The sky was a deep shade of gray, matching the heaviness of the Booker family's hearts.

Matty stood by the graveside clutching Jo Ann's hand on one side and his grandmother's hand on the other. Both quietly had tears rolling down their cheeks, making him wonder if he should be crying as well. Then he glanced over at his grandfather who was staring somberly and stoically at Ace's coffin clenching his teeth.

Maybe crying is what women do. We men, however, are expected to be stoic and put on my Grandpa Hank public face.

On one hand, Matty felt a hollowness and emptiness like he had never felt before. He would never see his father again. A piece of his life was now missing. On the other hand, as he looked around at those who had come to pay their last respects, on top of his sadness, he felt a mixture of curiosity and trepidation. This was the first time he had experienced closeup the death of a loved one. He had not attended Ace's father's funeral because of school and since Ace's father had lived so far away. But they hadn't been that close anyway.

The cemetery was hushed and those in attendance were mostly people he didn't know. They stared at the picture of Ace on top of the closed coffin. What they had in common was somber faces, and when they did speak, they talked in hushed tones. The air hung heavy with a combination the smell of freshly cut grass and sadness.

He looked at both his mother and grandmother. Each wore a black dress, and their faces had pained expressions. Each seemed to be whispering a prayer.

The minister began to speak in a gentle voice, his words a mixture of sorrow and memories. Matty tried to listen but found concentration difficult, making many of the minister's remarks float over his head like wisps of smoke. As the minister spoke, more tears welled up in Jo Ann's eyes, and Matty felt a lump form in his own throat.

I will never see dad again.

The coffin was lowered, and Matty watched as people walked by, putting a dab of ceremonial dirt on it. Then they said their goodbyes with each other by shaking hands and hugging and then beginning to walk back to their cars until no one was left except the Booker family.

As Jo Ann began to walk away, she looked up and saw Herman and Ralph Pogue staring at her from the parking area.

How inappropriate. We're here to pay our respects to my husband, and they're here for an entirely different reason. Hypocritical pigs. I have no doubt, they'll be celebrating at their house tonight.

Jo Ann excused herself and walk over to where they were standing.

"Enjoying the show? I can't believe you have the nerve and bad manners to show up so you can show your ass on a day like this."

"We're not here to show our ass," Herman said.

"You sure as hell aren't here to show your respect."

"You're right. We just wanted to see what it would be like to say goodbye properly since the members of our family seem to just go missing and no bodies ever seem to turn up. But I guess we can rest easy knowing that the con artist who started it all is now gone. I wanted to personally see him go in the ground," Ralph said.

"Whatever conflict there's been between our families happened because your family instigated it. We didn't move here looking for trouble. It was all your doing. If your family is snakebit as a result, it's their own damned fault."

Tubby Butler had stayed behind and saw where this conversation could escalate and quickly get out of control, so he stepped in.

"I don't want to hear another word out of either one of you. Now I want each of you to get in your car and leave. This is not a request. It's an order."

Ralph shot Tubby the finger but did as he was told, and the Pogues drove away.

Tubby then turned to Jo Ann and said, "I meant what I said. I'm not going to tolerate any more crap out of either one of you. Take my advice and don't bait these rednecks. You don't have Ace here to defend you anymore, and you've got a son to think about."

"Only if they'll lay off of us. I'm not going to roll over and play dead for this white trash, and you can go and tell them that. And you can tell them who sent the message. I'm not sure why, but they're running behind so far on this vendetta that they started, and I'd advise them to cut their losses while they can. And you can tell them that message came from me as well."

CHAPTER 46

Tubby sighed as he drove along the day after the funeral. He wasn't legally obligated to go to Jo Ann's house, but he felt morally obligated to keep her abreast of new developments relevant to her and not just let her read about them in the press or have to call him and pry the information out of him.

My job used to be so simple compared to what it is now. I'd report in, drink a little coffee and have a donut or two, and then go out on patrol. I'd ride around a lot and possibly give out a speeding ticket or two. On a bad day maybe I'd have to settle a domestic dispute or arbitrate some minor disagreement between two neighbors. Or maybe a merchant would call me because he caught some kid shoplifting. I'd go home at the end of the day, and the wife would ask, "How was your day?" and I'd respond, "Same old, same old." We'd then have dinner and watch a little TV. But now it seems that every day brings with it a new crisis. God, why can't we go back to the way things used to be?

He drove up to the Booker residence, parked, and got out and knocked on the door. No one answered, but both cars were there, so he walked around the house and saw Jo Ann weeding a flowerbed. Her father had given her the day off of work so she could spend some time alone. She had told Matty that she'd talk to Principal Dailey and get him an excused absence from school that day, but Matty declined her offer, saying he had a big test he really needed to take.

Jo Ann saw him, and said, "Oh, hi, Tubby. I didn't expect to see you today."

"I wish you didn't have to. I really feel bad about invading your privacy while you grieve, but something's come up that I think you should know about."

"Nothing's wrong with Matty, is it? Is that Pogue delinquent picking on him at school? If so, I'll make all of the whole bunch wish they were never born."

"Don't jump to conclusions, but this does involve the Pogue family. Last night someone killed both Herman and Ralph."

"I hope you're not here to accuse me of it. What happened?"

Tubby pulled up a folding aluminum chair and sat down. Jo Ann stopped weeding, took off her garden gloves, and pulled up another weed a few feet away from him.

"The two Pogue brothers went out to the Bootin' Scootin' Barn last night. You know, the honkytonk that has live music and where they do line dancing."

"Never been there, but I know the place you're talking about. I've heard it's a real scuzzy place."

"We do get a few calls to go out there."

"What were they doing? Celebrating Ace's death?"

"Probably."

"You damned well know so. They may have made a little money, but low-life white trash is low-life white trash no matter how much money they have. You can't buy class except for the kind they have — low. So, what happened?"

"Somebody killed both of them in the parking lot about eleven last night as they were leaving. Their waitress told me they were both pretty drunk and had been flashing bankrolls around that were the size of their fist. Anyway, they were both shot in the head at close range. They were both killed with the same gun — a pistol. The waitress said that there were several members of an out of town biker gang in there that night. Really rough looking characters. My theory is that when those bikers saw the Pogues flashing their money around and saw how drunk they both were, they decided to take advantage of the situation. What makes me think that even more is all of their cash was gone. Somebody sliced open the front pocket on each of their jeans. They weren't real careful about what they cut. Both Herman and Ralph had a pretty deep gash in their leg. The sheriff thinks it's a good probability it was the bikers."

"Sounds like it. But no one in the bar heard the shots? ... Or saw the shooter? That's hard to believe."

"Not really. The parking lot was full, ... party was still going strong ... and the Pogues had parked in the plumbing company's parking lot next door. Bootin' Scootin' uses it for overflow parking since they're closed at night. And you know the band gets pretty loud. We get complaints about the noise all the time. And don't forget, I'm sure most of the patrons were shit-faced, and their attention was on dancing. No, I'm not surprised at all."

"Well, don't expect me to shed any tears. They may have been tasteless enough to invade Ace's funeral service, but I wouldn't be caught dead at either one of theirs."

She looked up at the sky and said, "Thank you, God. You punish the wicked and believe in justice after all."

"The reason I'm here is not to give you an excuse to celebrate but to tell you this makes me concerned for you and Matty's safety. One of the surviving members of that crazy family might think you were somehow involved and come after both of you. You know, maybe they might think you hired a killer to do the job for you. I'll be close patrolling you for the immediate future."

"Thanks for thinking about us. You're right. They're just crazy enough to try to pull something."

Tubby nodded in agreement.

"So, y'all have no idea who pulled the trigger.?"

"I have my own theory. FDLE tells me that that Robert Perkins who's been hanging around in the county is a notorious professional killer they've want to nail for years. And if you'll remember, the Pogues trashed his truck with septic tank sludge. As a rule, People like him don't take things like that lying down. That's just not the way his kind does things. They've been known to kill people for less.

"Well, Perkins seems to have just disappeared. Personally, I think he assassinated the Pogues and then took off. On top of that, FDLE tells me the caliber of the pistol matches one that at one time was registered to him. I'm positive he's the man we want.

"FDLE has put out an APB statewide on him. We have his tag number and know what his truck looks like. It'll just be a matter of time until we nail the bastard. Believe me when I say he's finally going to get what's coming to him. He's been pretty cagy up till now, but he's finally slipped up, and we'll be able to send this sociopath to the chair where he belongs."

"I know you didn't have to tell me all this since it's an open investigation, but thanks."

"Your family has been through enough. But, Jo Ann, I'm not kidding. Watch your back, and don't let Matty put himself in a position where he's vulnerable. These people won't hesitate to use him to get even with you. That's just the kind of people they are. And I can only do so much."

CHAPTER 47

Tubby was true to his word in every way. On several occasions Jo Ann looked out the front window over the course of the week that followed and saw Tubby's patrol car slowly cruising by with him looking out the window to see if anything looked irregular. She saw other patrol cars from time to time as well.

She heard through the grapevine that Principal Dailey's secretary told some people that Tubby had visited the principal's office and told him that he expected to be kept informed if anyone started to bully or otherwise bother Matty and warned him that there would be ramifications if he failed to do so.

The following week, there was a knock at the door. When Jo Ann answered it, Tubby asked if he could come in.

"How are you adjusting? What about Matty? Is there anything you need me to do? I told you I'd keep you informed of any updates on finding Robert Perkins, Herman and Ralph's suspected killer. His truck was found abandoned in Macon, Georgia. At my request, I had them dust it for fingerprints. It had been wiped clean. Unfortunately, Perkins left no trail as where he might be heading. I had local authorities check various means of transportation such as the airport or the bus terminal, but they turned up nothing. I guess I shouldn't be totally surprised. The man's a professional. If anything else turns up, I'll keep you posted."

At first, Tubby gave Jo Ann as weekly courtesy visit, but as time went on they became less and less frequent.

Thanks to the support Jo Ann received from her parents, her life slowly returned to normal until the beginning of the following month. When Jo Ann got home from work, she found a Priority Mail envelope in her mailbox. The return address was Raleigh, North Carolina. When she opened it and reached in, she found six American Eagle $50 gold pieces. They were identical to the American Eagle coins she had found on the bedside table the day Ace died.

Jo Ann went on her computer to find out what she could about the return address on the envelope and was able to trace it to a woman. She then paid to get the woman's phone number.

"Ms. Scott ... My name is Jo Ann ..."

"Whatever you're selling, I don't want it."

"I'm not selling anything."

"Then whatever cause you're trying to get me to give money for, you can forget it."

"I'm just calling to see if you can help me with a personal matter. It doesn't involve money. Did you recently use Priority Mail to send something to Florida?"

"I don't have any idea what you're talking about. I know no one in Florida."

"Did someone else ask you to mail something to Florida?"

"No. How many times to I have to say it. I don't know a soul in Florida."

"That's all the information I need. Thank you very much for helping me out. And I apologize for disturbing you. I hope you have a wonderful day. Goodbye now. And thank you again."

Jo Ann hung up and sat silently as she replayed the conversation. Whoever sent the package had used a fake return address. She then decided that she'd tell no one, not even Matty.

At the beginning of the following month another Priority Mail package was delivered. It also had six American Eagle $50 gold pieces. This time the return address was Jackson, Mississippi. When she tried to track down the person sending it, it turned out to be a vacant lot.

The next month would have been Jo Ann and Ace's anniversary. The usual package arrived, this time from Kansas City, Missouri. Instead of the normal six coins, it contained seven. The return address turned out to be that of a mall. She still hadn't told anyone about her monthly windfalls. She simply took the coins and put them in a safety deposit box she had opened for herself at her father's bank.

The following month her mystery package arrived from Pasadena. California. Her investigation showed that the return address didn't even exist. The number of coins in the package had dropped back to six once again. She had had some extra expenses that month so she drove over to Panama City and sold one coin to a pawn shop.

After that, Jo Ann didn't even bother look up the return addresses on the envelopes any longer. She wasn't going to find out anything anyway. She simply dropped the coins silently in to the safety deposit box she was using as a savings mechanism. Topeka, Kansas. Austin, Texas. Denver. Colorado. San Antonio, Texas. Each month the package contained six coins with the exception of three months. On the month of her birthday, it once again increased to seven. It went again to seven the month Matty had his birthday. In December, it went to eight. She assumed this was because of Christmas.

In January, the pattern changed. This time the package was from the Cayman National Bank on Grand Cayman. There was no note of explanation in the envelope, just the usual six gold coins. Jo Ann went on-line. The Cayman National Bank was definitely for real. In fact, it was the largest bank in the Cayman Islands. The package did not have a specific banker's name. Her attempts at follow up only revealed what she already knew — that the Cayman Islands had very strict secrecy laws and that as a result it had become very popular in off-shore banking circles.

Each following month, the package continued to come from Cayman National. Each envelope always had the usual six gold coins except for months where she had a special event. The number of coins on these months were increased to the same level that they had been on the same month of the previous year, only to drop back again to six the following month.

Jo Ann continued to keep the packages a secret, even from Matty, and simply kept on depositing them in the safety deposit box. They were beginning to mount up. Occasionally when she needed extra money if she needed to do something like pay off a credit card, she would sell one through a pawn shop, being careful not to use the same pawn shop in the same city sequentially. Once she covered an usually high dental bill with the sale of a coin.

Now there was an additional reason to remain silent. She had never declared any of the coins or sales for tax purposes. She began to wonder just how long this largess would continue. There were never any notes of explanation or any accompanying paperwork. The pattern never changed.

When the school term ended, Jo Ann asked her father is she could have some vacation time.

"Of course," Hank replied. "Are you going anywhere, or are you just going to stay home?"

"I think Matty and I need to get away and just have some mother-son time."

"I'm glad. You know in the not too distant future, Matty's going to graduate from high school and go off to college. And who knows where he'll go after that. You'll regret that you didn't make more memories together while you had the chance. I've often wished that we had spent more time as a family. I just wish that Ace was still a part of the equation."

"In a strange sense, to me he still is and I hope always will be."

"Not being nosy or pushy, but you do know that if you want your mother and me to go somewhere with you, all you have to do is ask. Or if you want to go somewhere alone, Matty can stay with us until you get back."

"Thanks for the offers, dad."

"Got some place in particular in mind?"

"I'm thinking Grand Cayman, and this time I think Matty and I want to go down there just the two of us. I've never been there before."

"Good choice. Beautiful island. And a good time of year, before hurricane season gets seriously underway around here. It's also a slow time here at the bank. I hope you two just relax and have a wonderful time. You deserve it."

Jo Ann called Melinda Wurpts, a travel agent who banked at the Paradise Savings Bank. She told Melinda that she wanted a really nice hotel. Melina recommended the Hotel Indigo. She told Jo Ann that it was one of Grand Cayman's newer resorts and was right on Seven Mile Beach. It would have all the amenities that Jo Ann and Matty wanted. She would get them a two-bedroom suite with an ocean view. They set some dates, and Melinda began to make both the airline and the hotel reservations.

Once all the reservations had been made, Jo Ann and Matty flew to Miami and the caught the Cayman Airways flight out. They landed at 1:35 PM. Owen Roberts International Airport had a massive domed middle with an open-air observation "waving gallery" and was flanked by impressive low-slung connecting buildings, one each side. They then caught a cab to their hotel.

Seven Mile Beach, north of George Town, was a long crescent of coral-sand that has long been regarded by many as being the best beach in the Caribbean.

The hotel was everything that Melinda had said it would be. It was effervescent pink and had been decorated with an abundance of local artwork. There was no shortage of hotel restaurants. Their suite had a sunset view and overlooked an immaculate pool deck rife with chairs, umbrellas and towels. The infinity swimming pool was surrounded by an abundance of tall palm trees.

The following morning after they'd eaten breakfast Jo Ann told Matty she needed to take care of something in George Town and asked if he would mind just hanging out at the hotel until she got back. She suggested that he try the pool.

Jo Ann caught a cab to the Cayman National Bank. She purposely didn't make an appointment. First of all, she didn't know who to make an appointment with and second, she figured they'd have a harder time blowing her off if she was there in person rather than on the phone.

She walked in and was met by an bottom-rung banker who asked what her business was. She said she needed to talk to someone higher up. The lady offered to help, but Jo Ann told her that she'd prefer to talk to someone of authority since it was an issue of some importance. After waiting for thirty minutes, she was shown into a private office.

"My name is Mr. Billingsworth. And who do I have the pleasure of addressing?"

"My name is Jo Ann Booker or if you prefer Mrs. Matthew Booker. I'm a widow."

"Do you have an account with us? If so, I hope there isn't a problem with it."

"To tell you the truth, Mr. Billingsworth, I don't know if I have an account or not.

"Every month I get an envelope from the Cayman National Bank with American Eagle gold coins in it. There are usually six coins in the envelope, but that number sometimes varies. There is never any explanation or statement, only the coins. I'm here to get you to tell me what you know about it. First of all, who are they from?"

"Mrs. Booker, I am familiar with this transaction. It's one of the most unusual things we've ever been asked to do since I've worked here. And I've been here quite a while."

"Let me repeat, who are they from?"

"Unfortunately I can't disclose that fact. The client pays us a management fee as if it were an investment account, but we are not allowed to invest it. We are merely a custodian for the coins. And we're only allowed to take from it the disbursements you have described. They're paying us a lot of money to just mail an envelope once a month and provide safe storage for the remaining coins."

"What's the name on the account?"

"I am not allowed to disclose that fact either. You know, Cayman privacy laws. That's often why we're chosen by offshore banking clients."

"Can you tell me how long this arrangement is scheduled to go on?"

"No. But I will tell you this, at the risk of my job, if the current distribution rate continues, it will be a long time from now."

"But you won't tell me who the client is."

"Once again, I'm sorry, but no. I will tell you this much, however. To my knowledge no one in the bank has ever met the client. The account was set up by an attorney who has a power of attorney over it, and he sends us instructions each month as to the amount of that month's distribution."

"A local attorney?"

"No ... An American. I can't disclose where in the U.S., and I'm not even sure his practice is in the U.S. We communicate with a P.O. box. I would suggest that you simply enjoy your windfall, however long it continues to come. Is there anything else?"

"No, I don't guess there is. Thank you for your time, Mr. Billingsworth. And thank you for telling as much as you did. Don't worry about repercussions. This conversation will remain confidential."

"Thank you. If that's all, Mrs. Booker, I hope your visit to Grand Cayman is an enjoyable one and that you will visit us again in the future."

Jo Ann and Matty had a wonderful week on Grand Cayman. She returned with her questions still being unanswered but feeling somewhat secure anyway.

On the first day of the following month, six coins arrived right on schedule.

Jo Ann thought as she opened the safety deposit box to safeguard them, *The old adage says, 'If it ain't broke, don't fix it.' Well, sometimes it may be broke, and you can't fix it.*

This was followed by a second thought as she relocked the box.

Even in brokenness there's strength even if you've been snakebit if you simply suck it up and move on.

THE END

Thank you for reading.
Please review this book. Reviews
help others find Absolutely Amazing eBooks and
inspire us to keep providing these marvelous tales.
If you would like to be put on our email list
to receive updates on new releases,
contests, and promotions, please go to
AbsolutelyAmazingEbooks.com and sign up.

ABOUT THE AUTHOR

David Beckwith is a three-generation native of Greenville, Mississippi, with a BBA and an MBA from Ole Miss. His parents owned an independent cash commodity trading firm which also cleared securities trades through Goodbody & Co. David spent 40 years in the securities business, the first half of his career with Bache & Co. and its successors, the second half with Morgan Stanley. He retired as a Senior Vice President with approximately $500 million in responsibilities. For 25 years he has served as an adjunct professor at five different universities.

His first book was a narrative nonfiction work published by the University of Alabama Press in 2009 entitled *A New Day In The Delta*. The Mississippi Institute of Arts and Letters chose it as the runner-up for nonfiction book of the year. The book is often compared to Pat Conroy's *The Water Is Wide*. David started writing the Will and Betsy Black Adventure Series in 2010.

Moving to Key West, David Beckwith was tapped to write a book review column for the Keys *Citizen*, which David continues to produce on a weekly basis.

For sales, editorial information, subsidiary rights information
or a catalog, please write or phone or e-mail
Absolutely Amazing Books
Manhanset House
Shelter Island Hts., New York 11965-0342, US
Tel: 212-427-7139
www.absolutelyamazingebooks.com
bricktower@aol.com
www.IngramContent.com

www.ingramcontent.com/pod-product-compliance
Lightning Source LLC
Chambersburg PA
CBHW071435260626
47170CB00008B/2726